His Name Everywhere

A Legal Suspense Thriller

Howard Kane

Hidden Alpha Capital LLC

About the author

Howard Kane writes the stories most people are afraid to tell.

As a former Fortune 500 executive, he knows what it feels like to appear successful on the outside while quietly unraveling on the inside. For years, he hid his drinking behind late nights, busy calendars, and a polished smile. When he finally faced the truth about his addiction, he discovered that recovery wasn't just possible; it was life-changing.

Howard channels that experience into memoir-style novels that explore addiction, family trauma, money, and power. His five-book saga, The Daughter of a Drunk, follows Olivia Parker from a terrified little girl in a small Ohio town, vowing she'll never be like her father, to a woman fighting billionaires, corrupt institutions, and her own worst impulses. The series blends coming-of-age drama, generational alcoholism, and high-stakes whistleblower suspense into one continuous, bingeable story.

He also writes standalone novels rooted in alcohol dependence and recovery, including The Double Life of a High-Functioning Alcoholic, which pulls back the curtain on the addiction that hides behind ambition and success, and From Wine Mom to Sober Mom, which shines a light on the unique struggles mothers face when drinking threatens everything they love.

Through raw honesty and lived experience, Howard's books show that surviving a drunk parent or being the drunk parent is only the beginning. The real story is what you do with the wreckage. Readers describe his work as "impossible to put down" because the characters feel uncomfortably real, and their choices never come cheap.

If you've ever questioned your relationship with drinking, grown up in the shadow of someone else's, or wondered how far you'd go to protect the people you love, Howard Kane's stories are for you.

Website: https://selfcarejourneybooks.com/

Contents

Chapter One

Run

TWENTY MINUTES. THAT'S WHAT Griffin said. Twenty minutes until he arrived. Until we had to decide. Until everything changed. My hands wouldn't stop shaking. I stood at the window, watching the surveillance car parked across the street. The man inside hadn't moved in three hours. Hadn't left. Just sat there in the dark, waiting.

My phone buzzed. Text from Miranda: *Board vote moved to 2 PM tomorrow. Be safe.* Tomorrow. The vote that would determine if Noreen controlled Titan Capital. If my position stayed protected. If any of this mattered. But first, we had to survive tonight.

Grace came downstairs, rubbing her eyes. "Mama? Why are you standing there?"

"Just looking outside, baby."

"At what?"

"The sky. It's pretty tonight."

She came to the window and looked out. Didn't see the surveillance car. Didn't see the threat. Just saw darkness and streetlights and normal things. "I don't see sky. Just dark."

"You're right. It is dark." I picked her up. "Let's get back to bed."

"Not tired."

"I know. But you need to rest."

Linda appeared at the top of the stairs, understanding without words. "Come on, sweet pea. I'll read you another story."

"Two stories?"

"Three if you're good."

Grace went with Linda, trusting and safe, while I stood at the window counting minutes.

Noreen was on her phone, pacing the living room, her voice low and urgent. "I don't care what time it is. Call every board member. Tell them the FBI raided Margaret. Tell them we have evidence. Tell them—" She stopped. "Then make them listen."

She hung up and looked at me. "Half the board doesn't believe Steve's evidence is real. They think it's fake. Made up to hurt Margaret."

"It's not fake. You saw it."

"I know. But they haven't seen it. And without seeing it, they think this is just activist drama." She sat down heavily. "If I lose the vote tomorrow, Roth liquidates. Your position disappears. All the protection we built vanishes."

"And Margaret wins."

"And Margaret wins." Noreen's voice was bitter. "Even from jail. Even after everything. She still wins."

Headlights turned onto our street. I tensed and watched. A dark sedan pulled up slowly and stopped three houses down.

"That's not Griffin," I said.

Noreen came to the window. "How do you know?"

"Because Griffin said twenty minutes. It's only been twelve."

The sedan's engine stayed running. No one got out. The surveillance car flashed its lights. Once. Twice. The sedan flashed back.

"They're signaling each other," Noreen said. "Coordinating."

My chest tightened. "We need to leave. Now."

"Griffin said to wait—"

"I don't care what Griffin said. Margaret has two cars watching us. Maybe more. We're sitting targets," I said.

From the basement, a sound. Steve. Moaning. In pain. Linda came down the stairs quickly and quietly. "Steve's fever is spiking again. 104.2 F. He's not going to make it if we move him."

"He's not going to make it if we stay." I looked at the two cars outside, both waiting. "They're not surveillance. They're a kill team."

"You don't know that," Noreen said.

"Yes, I do." I thought about the warehouse and Keller's heart attack. "This is how Margaret works. She waits. She positions. Then she moves."

Another set of headlights. This one coming fast. FBI plates visible even in the dark. Griffin. He pulled up in front of our house, got out, suit, badge, gun visible. He walked to the door with purpose. I met him there, chain still on. "There are two other cars. One across the street. One three houses down. They were signaling each other."

Griffin's expression didn't change. "I know. I saw them."

"And?"

"And we need to move. Now. They're not FBI. They're not police. Which means they're Margaret's."

"How did they find us so fast?"

"Because Margaret owns half this town. Because Steve was right. She has people everywhere." Griffin looked past me. "Where's Adler?"

"Basement. Sick. Fever spiking."

"Can he walk?"

"Barely."

"Then we carry him." Griffin checked his watch. "We have maybe five minutes before they make their move. Maybe less."

Noreen stepped forward. "Who are you really? How do we know you're not one of Margaret's people?"

"You don't." Griffin pulled out his phone and showed her the screen. "But that's FBI Assistant Director Lee. I'm video calling him right now. You can verify I'm real, or you can stand here arguing while Margaret's people kick down your door."

He dialed. A man's face appeared. Asian, fifties, looking tired. "Griffin. Status?"

"At the Parker residence. Multiple hostiles outside. Requesting immediate extraction."

"Approved. Team is en route. ETA fourteen minutes."

"We don't have fourteen minutes."

"Then get them out. Go to your secondary location. We'll meet you there."

Griffin hung up and looked at me. "Your choice. Trust me or trust them." He pointed at the window. The surveillance car door was opening. The man getting out.

"Decide now."

I looked at Noreen, at Linda standing at the top of the stairs, at the basement door hiding Steve. I made a choice. Opened the door for Griffin to come in. "Linda, get Grace. Noreen, help me with Steve. We're leaving."

Everyone moved. Linda ran upstairs. I heard Grace protesting. "But Mama said—"

"I know, baby. Change of plans. We're going on an adventure."

Noreen and I went to the basement. Steve was conscious, barely. He saw us coming. "What's happening?"

"Margaret's people are outside. We're leaving."

"Can't. Too weak."

"You don't get a choice." I grabbed one arm, and Noreen grabbed the other. "We're carrying you." We pulled him up. He screamed, the wound tearing, blood soaking through the bandage. But he was up. We half-carried, half-dragged him upstairs. Each step was agony for him. Agony for us watching.

Griffin was at the front door, looking out the peephole. "They're coming. Both cars. Four men. Maybe five. Armed."

"Back door," Linda said. She had Grace, wrapped in a blanket, half-asleep and confused.

"They'll cover the back," Griffin said. "We go out the basement window to the side yard. My car's there."

"Your car's in front," I said.

"Not mine. My partner's. Unmarked. Gray Honda. Keys are under the mat."

We went back to the basement, moving quickly. Steve's weight made everything harder. Griffin broke the glass from the window, knocked out the frame, and made it bigger. "Ladies first."

Linda went through, Grace in her arms. I heard her land outside with a soft grunt. Noreen went next, faster and practiced, as if she'd done this before.

"Adler. You're next."

"Can't fit."

"You fit or you die. Choose." Steve tried. He got his head through, his shoulders, then got stuck. The wound and bandage were too bulky.

"Take it off," Griffin said. "The bandage. Take it off."

"He'll bleed out—"

"He'll die here if we don't move. Take it off."

I ripped off the bandage. Steve screamed. Blood everywhere, fresh and hot. But he fit through. We pushed. He screamed louder, the wound tearing, skin catching on broken glass. But he was through. Linda and Noreen caught him outside and held him up.

"Your turn," Griffin said to me.

"You first."

"I'm trained for this. You're not. Go."

I went through, scraping my side on glass. I felt blood but didn't care. I landed in dead grass, cold and dark. Griffin came last, just as we heard the front door crash open inside. Wood splintering. Men shouting.

"FBI! Come out with your hands up!"

Griffin smiled, cold. "Still pretending."

We ran through the side yard and into the alley. Griffin's partner's car was there: a gray Honda, ordinary and forgettable. Keys under the mat. Griffin got in the driver's seat and started the engine. I got in back with Steve and Noreen, while Linda and Grace were in front.

Behind us, men poured out of my house, three of them, guns drawn, looking for us. But we were already gone. Griffin pulled away smoothly, no screeching tires, no drama, just a gray Honda leaving an alley. It could have been anyone. One of the men saw us and raised his gun.

"Get down!" Griffin shouted. I pushed Steve down and covered Grace with my body. A shot. Glass shattered. The rear window exploded. Grace screamed. Griffin floored it. The Honda lurched forward, fast, faster, taking corners hard. Another shot hit the trunk, metal crunching. Then we were around the corner, gone, lost in the maze of Cleveland streets.

Grace was crying, full sobs, while Linda held her. "It's okay, baby. We're okay. You're okay." But she wasn't okay. None of us were okay. I looked at Steve. He was unconscious, blood pooling on the seat beneath him, the wound completely open now, nothing stopping it.

"He's going to die," I said.

"Not if I can help it." Griffin drove fast but not recklessly, taking random turns to ensure no one followed. "There's a trauma kit under your seat. Use it."

I found it. Military style. Packed with supplies: gauze, pressure bandages, clotting agents. I worked on Steve while Griffin drove, trying to stop the bleeding and keep him alive.

Noreen helped, holding pressure and following my instructions. Her hands were shaking but steady enough.

"Where are we going?" Linda asked, her voice too calm, the one that meant terror underneath.

"Safe house. Off the grid. Margaret doesn't know about it."

"How can you be sure?"

"Because I'm still alive." Griffin checked the mirror. "If Margaret knew where I lived or where I hid people, I'd be dead. Like Keller. Like everyone else who got close."

We drove out of the city, into darkness, country roads, no streetlights, no other cars. Grace had stopped crying, just hiccupping, exhausted and confused. Linda held her. "Sing with me, sweet pea. You know this one."

She started singing softly, some lullaby. Grace joined in with her tiny, broken voice. And somehow that made it worse, that beautiful broken singing while Steve bled and men hunted us, and everything fell apart.

Twenty minutes, that's how long we drove. Then Griffin turned onto a dirt road, trees closing in, dark and thick, no houses, no lights, nothing.

"Where are we?" Noreen asked.

"Nowhere, which is the point."

The cabin appeared, small, dark, hidden among the trees. Griffin pulled up and cut the engine. "We're here. Let's get Adler inside." We carried Steve; he was unconscious, dead-weight, leaving a blood trail behind us.

The cabin was one room, basic: bed, couch, kitchen, old furniture, everything worn but clean. We put Steve on the bed. Linda went to work immediately, checking vitals, stopping the bleeding, doing what nurses do when people are dying and there's nothing else to do but try. Griffin locked the door and checked the windows. "We're safe here. For tonight at least."

"And tomorrow?" I asked.

"Tomorrow we figure out what comes next."

He pulled out his phone and made a call. "Assistant Director Lee. We're at the secondary location. Safe. But Adler is critical. We need medical support."

He listened; his face remained unchanged. "Understood. Morning then. And Lee? We need a team. Full protection. Margaret knows they escaped. She'll be looking."

He hung up and looked at all of us. "FBI team arrives at dawn. Eight agents. Full tactical. Until then, we sit tight."

Grace was asleep in Linda's arms, exhausted, traumatized, but alive. Noreen sat in the corner, staring at nothing, phone in her hand. The board vote tomorrow, her father's company, everything on the line. Steve was unconscious, fever-sick, bleeding, maybe dying. And I stood in the middle of it all, watching my world break, watching everything I'd tried to protect fall apart.

Griffin brought me coffee. I didn't remember him making it, didn't remember him having a kitchen. "Drink. You need it."

I drank; it was terrible, too strong, too bitter, but hot, real. "Did we just make it worse?" I asked. "Running?"

"No. Staying would have been worse. Margaret sent a kill team. Not surveillance. Not watchers. People meant to clean up loose ends." He sat down. "You, Linda, Grace, Steve. All loose ends."

"And now?"

"Now you're under federal protection. Margaret can't touch you without declaring war on the FBI. She's not that stupid."

"Isn't she? She killed Keller. She tried to kill Steve. She doesn't care about the FBI."

"She cares about not dying in prison. Killing a protected witness? That's life without parole. She's too smart for that."

"But sending people to my house wasn't?"

Griffin was quiet. Then: "She's desperate. The FBI raid spooked her. She knows we're close. So she's moving fast. Trying to eliminate threats before we build the case."

"Did she eliminate Steve?"

We both looked at the bed. Linda was working. Steve was still. Too still.

"I don't know," Griffin said. "But if he dies, we need that evidence from Chicago. Without it, Margaret walks."

"He won't tell you where it is. He said he needs to be there."

"He doesn't get to make demands."

The room went quiet. Just Steve's ragged breathing. Grace's soft snoring. The wind outside. Noreen walked to the window. She stood next to Griffin. "The board votes at two tomorrow. I need to be there."

"That's a risk."

"Everything's a risk now." She looked at her phone. "Miranda says it's 50-50. Half the board wants to fight Margaret. Half wants to cut losses and run. I need to convince them."

"With what? Steve's evidence is in Chicago. You have samples. Margaret's lawyers will call them fake."

"I have Steve's testimony. His willingness to turn on Margaret. That means something."

"It means he's scared. It doesn't prove Margaret's guilty." Griffin turned to face her. "You need the full evidence. Bank records. Wire transfers. Margaret's signatures. Everything. Without it, your board votes to liquidate. Olivia loses protection. We all lose."

"Then we get Steve to Chicago."

"He can't travel. Look at him." We all looked. Steve was gray. Sweat-soaked. Dying, maybe.

"Then we go without him," Noreen said. "He tells us where the evidence is. We retrieve it. Bring it back."

"He won't do that."

"Make him. This is bigger than his paranoia. This is justice for my father. For everyone Margaret killed." Noreen's voice grew hard. "I'm not letting her win because Steve Adler doesn't trust the FBI."

"I'm standing right here." We all turned. Steve. Conscious. Barely. His voice was so weak I almost didn't hear it.

"And I heard every word. You want the evidence? Fine. But I'm not telling you where it is. I'm not giving you the passwords. I'm not trusting the FBI with everything until I know I'm safe."

"You're under federal protection—"

"Keller was under protection. He's dead." Steve coughed, blood on his lips. "I'm not dying before I see Margaret in prison. That's the deal. You keep me alive until I testify. Until she's convicted. Then I'll give you everything."

"That's not how this works—"

"That's how it works now." Steve's eyes found mine. "Olivia understands. She knows. Trust gets you killed. The only currency left is leverage. I have leverage. That's why I'm still breathing." He closed his eyes and passed out again.

Linda came over. "His fever's dropping. One-oh-two point eight. The antibiotics are working. Slowly, but working."

"How long until he can travel?" Griffin asked.

"A week. Maybe more."

"We don't have a week."

"Then he dies. Choose." Linda's voice was flat. "You push him to travel, you kill him. His wound will open. He'll get septic. He'll die before you get him to Chicago."

Griffin swore quietly, viciously. Noreen pulled out her phone. "I'm calling Miranda. Telling her I'm flying back for the vote tomorrow morning. If I miss it, we lose everything."

"Margaret will be looking for you—"

"So I'll be careful. I'll use private security. I'll take precautions." Noreen looked at me. "But I'm not losing my father's company because I'm scared. That's not who I am." She went outside to make the call, letting the door close softly behind her.

Linda put Grace on the couch and covered her with a blanket. "She's exhausted. Traumatized. But she'll sleep."

"Will she be okay?" I asked.

"I don't know. She watched men break into our house, heard gunshots, ran through the night. She's three." Linda sat down heavily. "But she's strong. Like you. She'll survive."

Griffin's phone buzzed. He checked it. "My team is in position. Eight agents forming a perimeter around this property. No one gets in without us knowing."

"What about getting out?" I asked.

"That's up to you. You want to run? Run. I won't stop you. But Margaret will find you. She always does. Or you stay here. Let us protect you. Let us build the case. Let us put her away."

"And if Steve dies before he tells us where the evidence is?"

"Then we improvise. Find other witnesses. Build a circumstantial case. It's not perfect, but it's something."

"Something isn't justice."

"No. But sometimes something is all we get."

I looked around the cabin. One room. Five people. Hunted. Scared. Hoping the FBI could protect us. Hoping Steve lived long enough to testify. Hoping Margaret didn't find us first.

Outside, dawn was coming. Gray light filtered through the trees. The first birds sang. The world woke up as if nothing was wrong. As if people's lives weren't shattering. As if justice wasn't hanging by a thread.

Chapter Two

The Cabin

GRACE WOKE UP CRYING. Not screaming. Not the nightmares she used to have. Just quiet tears rolling down her face while she stared at the unfamiliar ceiling. "Mama?"

I was already there. I had been watching her sleep for the past hour, making sure she was breathing, making sure this was real. "I'm here, baby."

"Where are we?"

"A safe place. A friend's house."

"Why?"

"Because some bad people were at our house. So we came here."

Grace sat up and looked around the cabin. One room. Strange furniture. Windows showing trees instead of the street. Morning light coming through dirty glass. Nothing familiar. Nothing safe. "My toys?"

The question broke me. Her favorite things. The stuffed elephant Linda gave her. The blocks Leo bought before he died. The books we read every night. All left behind. All gone. "At home. We'll get them soon."

"When?"

"I don't know."

Her face crumpled, lower lip trembling, eyes filling with tears again. "I wanna go home."

"I know, baby. Me too."

Linda appeared from the kitchen corner. She had been making coffee on Griffin's ancient stove. The smell filled the cabin. Strong. Bitter. Real. "Morning, sweet pea. Hungry?"

Grace nodded, wiping her eyes with the back of her hand.

"Well, this house doesn't have your favorite cereal. But we have toast. And I found some jam."

"Strawberry jam?"

"Grape. Is that okay?"

Grace considered this. Serious. Like it was the biggest decision in the world. Then she nodded. Simple. Three years old. Just wanted strawberry jam and her toys and to go home. I watched her eat. Toast cut into triangles. Purple jam smeared on her face. Happy for this one small normal thing.

Outside, voices. Griffin talking to his team. They'd arrived at dawn like he promised. Eight FBI agents. Two SUVs. Setting up a perimeter around the cabin. Making us safe. Supposedly.

Steve was still unconscious on the bed. Fever down slightly from last night. 102.5 F. Better than the 104 F he'd been running. But his wound kept seeping, blood soaking through the fresh bandage Linda had just changed an hour ago.

Noreen sat in the corner chair, still wearing yesterday's clothes. Hair pulled back. No makeup. She looked younger without it. Vulnerable. Hadn't slept. Just stared at nothing while her phone sat in her lap, waiting for news from New York. The board vote, originally scheduled for 2 PM today. But that felt like a lifetime away. Everything felt far away. Unreal.

Griffin came back inside, bringing cold air with him. He closed the door softly so Grace wouldn't notice. "My team is fully deployed. Two agents at the road. Two in the woods on each side. Two with the vehicles. Full communications. Motion sensors on the perimeter." He poured coffee, black, no sugar. "We're as safe as we can be out here."

"How long can we stay?" I asked.

"Long as we need. This place is off the grid. No utilities in my name. No paper trail. Cash purchase ten years ago." He glanced at Steve. "How is he?"

"Fever's down. But he's still unconscious. The wound keeps bleeding."

"Can he travel to Chicago?"

"Not for at least a week. Maybe more."

Griffin swore, quietly but viciously. "We don't have a week. Margaret's already looking. Every hour Steve stays hidden is one more hour she searches."

"So what do we do?"

"We get him stable enough to talk. Get the information about Chicago. Then we go get the evidence ourselves."

"He won't tell you. He said last night—"

"I know what he said. But he doesn't get to make demands. This is a federal investigation. He cooperates or we leave him to Margaret." The words hung there, cold and true.

Noreen's phone rang. She looked at the screen and answered quickly. "Miranda. What's wrong?" She listened. Her face changed, color draining, eyes going wide.

"When? How many votes?" Pause. "Are you sure? Completely sure?" She hung up and looked at us. "Emergency board meeting. Nine AM instead of two PM. Roth called it."

"Why?" Griffin asked.

"He says he has new information. Claims my father was killed because of illegal activities. Says the fund is at risk if I take over. Says I'm too emotionally compromised to lead." Her voice grew hard and angry. "He's trying to force the vote before I can get there. Before I can defend myself."

"That's in ninety minutes," I said, checking the clock. 7:36 AM.

"I know." Noreen stood and grabbed her jacket. "I need to get to New York. Now. Or I lose everything."

Griffin pulled out his phone. "Okay then, I'll call for transport. Helicopter from Burke Lakefront. Can have you in the air in forty minutes."

"Do it."

He stepped outside, making calls and coordinating. A few minutes later, Griffin came back in. "Helicopter's waiting at Burke Lakefront Airport. We leave in five minutes."

"Okay." Noreen looked at Grace, at Linda, at Steve unconscious on the bed. "You'll be safe here. Griffin's team is good. They'll protect you."

"Go. Win the vote. We'll be fine."

She hesitated, then nodded and grabbed her things. Griffin looked at me. "I'll be back in two hours. Three at most. My team stays here. They have orders. Nobody gets near this cabin."

"What about Margaret?"

"She doesn't know about this place. She's looking in Cleveland, at hotels, at known safe houses. Not here." He checked his weapon. "But if something happens... if my team tells you to move, you move. No questions. Understood?"

"Understood."

He and Noreen left, the engine starting and gravel crunching under tires. Then they were gone. And we were alone: me, Linda, Grace, Steve, and eight FBI agents in the woods. The cabin felt smaller without them, quieter; the walls seemed closer.

Grace finished her toast, purple jam on her chin. "Mama, can I go outside?"

"Not right now, baby."

"Why?"

"Because we're staying inside today. It's safer."

"But I wanna play outside."

"I know. Maybe tomorrow."

Her face crumpled again. "You always say tomorrow." The words hit hard. True. I'd been saying tomorrow for months. Tomorrow we'll go to the park. Tomorrow we'll visit the zoo. Tomorrow things will be normal. Tomorrow never came.

"I'm sorry, baby. I know it's hard."

"I don't like this place. I want to go home."

"Me too."

She started crying. Real tears. Not just upset. Scared. Overwhelmed. Three years old and her whole world had shattered. Linda picked her up. "Hey, sweet pea. It's okay. Everything's okay."

"No, it's not. Bad people came. We ran away. Mama's sad. I want my toys." She sobbed into Linda's shoulder. "I want to go home."

I felt it breaking. The thing inside me that had held together through everything. Through Leo's death. Through the warehouse. Through Tyler's trial. Through Margaret's threats. Through last night's escape. Breaking. Grace crying. Steve dying. Noreen fighting for control. Griffin gone. Us hiding in a cabin while Margaret hunted us. All of it crashing down.

I went to the bathroom. Small. Cramped. Mirror cracked. Closed the door. Sat on the floor. And cried. Not quiet tears.

Not dignified grief. Full-body sobs. The kind that shake you. The kind that hurt. Grace deserved better. Deserved normal. Deserved a mother who wasn't hunted. Who wasn't broken. Who didn't drag her daughter into war zones. But this was all I had. All I could give her. Running, hiding, and hoping we survived.

A knock on the door. Linda's voice. "Olivia? You okay?"

"Yeah. Just need a minute."

"Take your time. Grace is watching cartoons on my phone. She's okay."

I washed my face. Cold water. Looking in the cracked mirror at someone I barely recognized. Exhausted. Scared. Barely holding on. But still standing. Still fighting. That had to be enough. I went back out. Grace was cuddled with Linda on the couch. Watching some cartoon. Calm now. The storm had passed. "Sorry, baby. Mama just needed to wash her face."

"You okay?"

"Yeah. I'm okay."

She went back to the cartoon. Believing me. Trusting me. Like three-year-olds do. I checked on Steve. Temperature the same. 102.5 F. Wound still seeping. But breathing steady. Still alive. Linda came over. Quiet. "How are you really?"

"Tired. Scared. Wondering if we're going to make it."

"We will."

"You don't know that."

"No. But I believe it. And sometimes belief is all we have."

The morning dragged. Minutes crawled by. Grace watching cartoons. Linda reading an old magazine she found. Me checking on Steve. Listening for sounds that didn't belong.

At 9:47 AM, my phone rang. Noreen. "Did you make it?" I answered.

"Barely. Helicopter got me here with five minutes to spare." Her voice was tight. Stressed. "The meeting starts in ten minutes. Roth presented his case for why I'm unfit. Now I get to respond."

"What did he say?"

"That my father was reckless. That he died because he took unnecessary risks. That I'm too emotional and revenge-driven to lead the fund. That I'll destroy everything he built chasing Margaret." She paused. "He's not completely wrong."

"He's completely wrong."

"Maybe. But he convinced three board members. I need to win them back. Or I lose."

"Then convince them. Show them Steve's evidence. Show them what Margaret did. Show them your father died a hero."

"I'm trying. But Olivia—" Her voice cracked. "I'm terrified. If I lose this, everything my father built disappears. Everything he died for becomes meaningless."

"Then don't lose."

"It's not that simple—"

"Yes, it is. Go in there. Tell them the truth. Win." My voice grew more forceful. "Because if you lose, your father dies for nothing. And Margaret wins. So don't lose."

Silence. Then: "Okay. I won't lose."

"Good luck."

"I don't believe in luck. But thank you." She hung up.

I went back to the window. Trees. FBI agents moving through the woods. The perimeter keeping us safe. For now.

10:15 AM. Steve's temperature spiked. 103.2 F. I called Linda. She came over. Checked him. Her face tight. Professional mask cracking. "That's not good."

"How not good?"

"The infection's getting worse. Spreading. The antibiotics Dr. Walsh gave him aren't strong enough." She touched his forehead. Jerked her hand back. "He's burning up."

"What do we do?"

"Call Dr. Walsh. See if she has stronger antibiotics. Or—" Linda didn't finish.

"Or what?"

"Or we take him to a hospital. Before the infection goes septic." Septic. Blood infection. Organ failure. Death.

I called Dr. Walsh. Explained the situation. Rising fever. Wound getting worse. Blood seeping through bandages. She was quiet. "That's sepsis. Early stage. But it'll progress fast."

"Can you bring stronger antibiotics?"

"Not strong enough. He needs IV antibiotics. Hospital-grade. Monitoring every few hours." Her voice became firm. "Without a hospital, he'll die. Probably within 24 hours."

My stomach dropped. "We can't take him to a hospital. Margaret—"

"Will kill him anyway if the infection goes septic. At least a hospital gives him a chance."

"She has people everywhere. She'll find out."

"Metro Hospital has a secure wing. Federal witness protection. They handle cases like this. They'll know how to keep him safe." She paused. "But you need to decide fast. Every hour you wait makes it worse." She hung up.

I went back to Steve. Touched his shoulder. Hot. Too hot. "Steve. Wake up." His eyes opened. Barely. Glassy with fever.

"You're very sick. We need to take you to the hospital."

His eyes focused suddenly. Fear cutting through the fever. "No."

"You'll die without treatment."

"No hospital." He tried to sit up. Couldn't. Too weak. "Margaret... she'll know... she's watching hospitals..."

"We'll use a secure wing. Federal witness protection. She can't get to you there."

"She always finds out. Always." His hand grabbed my wrist. Burning hot. Desperate. "Can't go. She'll know. She'll come. She'll find Grace..."

"Steve, you're dying."

"Better than... leading Margaret here... to your daughter..." He was barely coherent, fever-talking but adamant, certain. "No hospital. Let me die here... just don't... don't lead her to Grace..." His eyes closed, passing out again. Breathing rapidly, shallow. Skin gray.

Linda stood at the doorway. "He's refusing treatment."

"He's delirious. Fever talking."

"Maybe. But he's conscious. He's making a choice. A bad one. But it's his choice." She came down and checked his vitals. "We can't force him. That's assault. Kidnapping. Legally, he has the right to refuse."

"Even if he's dying?"

"Even then."

I wanted to scream, to shake Steve awake, to make him understand he was being stupid. That hospitals could protect him. That dying in a cabin accomplished nothing. But he was right about one thing. Margaret would find out. She had money, resources, people inside police departments, inside hospitals, and probably inside the FBI. If we took Steve to a hospital, she'd know within hours. And then she'd come. Not just for Steve. For all of us. For Grace.

I sat on the basement steps, head in my hands, trying to think, trying to find a solution that didn't end with everyone dead. Linda sat next to me. "What are you going to do?"

"I don't know."

"He's dying. Right now. In front of us. We have maybe twelve hours. Maybe less."

"I know."

"So we let him die? We just watch?"

"What choice do we have? He's refusing treatment. Margaret's hunting us. Griffin's gone. We're trapped." I looked at her. "What would you do?"

Linda was quiet for a long time. Then: "I'd save him. Hospital or not. Margaret or not. I'd save his life. Even when it's dangerous."

"And if that puts Grace in danger?"

"Then we failed. But at least we tried. At least we didn't give up."

She went back upstairs, leaving me alone with the choice: let Steve die, keep Grace safe, and hope Margaret never finds us. Or save Steve, risk everything, hope the hospital can protect us, hope Margaret doesn't find out, hope we survive. Some choice.

I went up to Grace. She was coloring now with crayons Griffin kept in a drawer, drawing flowers or something. Three-year-old art that looked like circles and lines. "Mama, look what I made."

"That's beautiful, baby."

"It's for you. So you won't be sad."

The words broke me. "Thank you, baby. I love it."

She went back to coloring, happy, safe, trusting me to protect her. I couldn't let Steve die. Couldn't watch him slip away while I did nothing. That wasn't who I was. That wasn't what Grace needed to see her mother be. I called Griffin. He answered on the second ring.

"What's wrong?"

"Steve's dying. Fever's spiking. Dr. Walsh says he needs a hospital or he'll die within 24 hours."

Griffin swore. "Steve's refusing?"

"Yes. Says Margaret will find out. That she'll come for Grace."

"He's probably right. But if he dies, the evidence dies with him. We lose everything."

"So what do I do?"

"You take him to the hospital. Metro has a secure wing. Federal witness protection. I'll call ahead and have agents waiting. Full security." He paused. "It's risky, but it's the only option."

"And if Margaret finds out?"

"Then we deal with it. At least Steve will be alive. At least we'll have a chance." His voice grew firm. "Call an ambulance. Secure transport. I'll coordinate from here. And Olivia?"

"Yeah?"

"You're doing the right thing. Steve's scared and paranoid, but saving his life is what matters." He hung up.

I went back downstairs. Steve was unconscious now, which changed things. I couldn't refuse treatment if he wasn't conscious to refuse. I made the call. "This is Olivia Parker. I'm at Griffin's cabin location. We have a federal witness in critical condition. We need secure transport to Metro Hospital."

The dispatcher was calm and professional. "Secure transport deploying. ETA fifteen minutes. Stay with the patient and keep him stable."

"Understood."

I hung up and looked at Steve. His skin was gray, his breathing rapid. He was dying. "I'm sorry, but I'm not letting you die. Not here. Not like this."

Linda came down. "You called an ambulance?"

"Yes."

"Good. He needs it." She checked his vitals. "Blood pressure's dropping. Pulse is weak. We don't have much time."

Grace appeared at the top of the stairs. "Mama? What's happening?"

"The sick man needs to go to the doctor. I'm going to go with him to make sure he's okay."

"You're leaving?" Her voice was small and scared.

"Just for a little while. Linda's staying with you."

Grace's eyes filled with tears. "But you just got here."

"I know, baby. I'm sorry, but I have to help."

"Okay." She went back to Linda without another word, her quiet acceptance hurting more than if she had cried. I wanted to go to her, hold her, and tell her everything would be okay.

But the ambulance was coming, Steve was dying, and time was running out.

The ambulance arrived at 11:03 AM. It wasn't a regular ambulance; it was an unmarked van with two paramedics in plain clothes. They came inside, saw Steve, and moved fast with no wasted motion. "We need to move now."

They got Steve on a stretcher, started an IV, and connected monitors and an oxygen mask, moving with practiced efficiency. Grace stood at the window, watching. "Is he going to die?"

The question cut through me. At three years old, she was already learning that people die, that mothers leave, that nothing stays safe. "I hope not, baby."

They loaded Steve into the van, and I got in as well. One of Griffin's agents got in too. Armed. Alert. Linda stood in the doorway with Grace. "Call me when you get there."

"I will."

"And Olivia? You're doing the right thing."

The doors closed, the engine started, and we pulled away. I watched the cabin disappear through the small window, Linda holding Grace, both waving, getting smaller, then gone. Steve stirred, his eyes opening slightly. "Hospital?"

"Yes."

"Margaret... will know..."

"I know. But you're alive. That's what matters."

"Grace... keep her safe..."

"I will."

His eyes closed. "Chicago... if I die... you have to get the evidence... don't let Margaret win..."

"You're not going to die."

"But if I do—"

"You won't. You're going to testify. You're going to watch Margaret go to prison."

He relaxed slightly. Stopped fighting. The paramedic checked the monitors. "BP is still dropping. We need to move faster." The van accelerated. Cleveland streets blurred past. Normal people living normal lives while we raced against death.

The hospital appeared. Metro Hospital. Large. Gray. Modern. Intimidating. We pulled into a side entrance. Service door marked "Authorized Personnel Only."

Two FBI agents were waiting. Suits. Badges. Weapons visible. They pulled Steve out. Moving fast. Through the door. Into an elevator. Up to the sixth floor. Through secure doors. Past the nurses' station. Into room 6-17.

Doctors were waiting. Three of them. Moving immediately. Checking vitals. Examining the wound. The lead doctor looked at the wound. Then at the monitors. His face tightened. "Advanced sepsis. Blood pressure critical. The wound is necrotic. We need surgery immediately."

"Will he survive?" I asked.

"Maybe. If we operate now. If the infection hasn't spread to major organs." He looked at me. "How long has he been this bad?"

"Fever started yesterday. Got worse this morning."

"You should have brought him in yesterday. Every hour matters with sepsis." He wasn't angry. Just stating facts. "But we'll do everything we can."

They wheeled Steve out. Down the hall. To the operating room. Moving fast. Urgent. And I stood in the empty room, watching them disappear. Watching Steve's life hang by a thread. The FBI agent touched my arm. "He's in good hands. Best surgeons in Cleveland. If anyone can save him, they can."

"And if they can't?"

"Then we lost a witness. And Margaret gets away with murder." He looked at me. "But we're not there yet. Adler's tough. He'll fight."

A nurse came in. Young. Kind face. "Surgery will take at least three hours. Possibly more if the infection has spread. You can wait in the family room down the hall." Three hours minimum. Maybe more. Just waiting. Hoping. Praying Steve survived.

I followed her to the family room. Uncomfortable chairs. Old magazines. TV playing news on mute. Fluorescent lights buzzing overhead. The FBI agent sat by the door. Watching. Alert. I called Linda. "We're at the hospital. Steve's in surgery."

"How bad?"

"Bad. Advanced sepsis. Necrotic wound. They're operating now. At least three hours."

"And you?"

"Waiting. Nothing else to do."

"Grace is okay. Playing with those crayons. Drew you six more pictures." Linda's voice softened. "She understands you had to go. She's braver than we give her credit for."

"Tell her I love her."

"I will. Call me when he's out of surgery."

"Okay." I hung up. Sat back in the uncomfortable chair. Watched the clock. 11:47 AM. Three hours meant 2:47 PM at the earliest. I leaned back and waited.

Chapter Three

Twenty-Four Hours

At 11:52 AM, Griffin came back to the hospital and handed me his phone with Noreen on the line.

"Noreen, how did the vote go?" I asked.

Silence. Then, "Roth won. 7-4." I closed my eyes.

"He presented Keller's FBI investigation as evidence of instability. Said the fund was at risk. Said I was too inexperienced." Her voice was flat. "The board voted for Roth."

"So he controls everything."

"Yes. But there's one piece of good news. The SEC investigation freezes all positions for six months. He can't liquidate your position. You're protected by federal law." Relief. Small but real.

"So the guarantee that David previously provided doesn't matter."

"It's irrelevant. You're protected either way." She paused. "But Roth controls the fund. Controls strategy. Controls whether we keep fighting Margaret."

"What does that mean?"

"It means he called me after the vote. Said he's considering a settlement with Margaret. Ending the fight. Walking away."

My blood went cold. "The FBI investigation continues though, right? That's criminal. That's separate from our proxy fight."

"Yes. The FBI proceeds either way. But here's the problem." Noreen's voice grew firmer. "Roth settling means Titan stops cooperating. Our forensic accountants who've been building the case? Gone. Our financial analysts who can verify Steve's documents? Gone. Our lawyers who've been coordinating with federal prosecutors?"

"But the FBI has Steve. Has his evidence."

"They have testimony from a confessed criminal who cooked Margaret's books for twelve years. Do you know what defense attorneys will do to him on the stand? 'Mr. Adler, didn't you commit fraud for twelve years? Didn't you lie routinely? Why should we believe you now?'" She paused.

"With Titan backing the case, we have independent verification. Financial experts who can say, 'Yes, these documents are authentic. Yes, this shows criminal activity.' Without us, it's Steve's word against Margaret's lawyers."

I looked at Griffin. He nodded grimly.

"Prosecutors look at cases they can win," Noreen continued. "Steve alone is risky. Steve plus institutional backing is prosecutable. Roth settling doesn't end the investigation, but it makes it a lot harder to get an indictment."

"When is Roth meeting with Margaret's lawyers?"

"Tomorrow afternoon. 2 PM. If they make the right offer, and she will, he'll take it."

"So we have less than 24 hours."

"To do what? Steve's in surgery. The evidence is wherever he hid it. We don't even know where."

"Chicago. Safe deposit box."

"Which bank? Which box number? Do you have a key?" Noreen's voice was sharp. "Because if Steve dies on that operating table, or if he's unconscious for the next 24 hours, none of that matters. Margaret wins by default."

My stomach turned over.

"There's something else," Noreen said. "Something worse."

"What?"

"Margaret knows Steve was taken to a hospital. She doesn't know which one yet, but she's looking. And the moment she realizes he's conscious, the moment she realizes he can tell people where the evidence is, she'll act."

"The evidence location. Olivia, think about it. Steve's been hiding for months. He's been careful. But Margaret's not stupid. She knows he'd hide evidence somewhere accessible, somewhere he could get to quickly if needed. She's probably already narrowed it down to major cities within a few hours of Cleveland: Chicago, Pittsburgh, Detroit. She's got people watching storage facilities, banks, anywhere someone might hide documents."

Griffin spoke up. "She's right. Margaret has resources: private investigators, former cops, people who know how to track paper trails."

"But she doesn't know the specific location," I said.

"Not yet," Noreen agreed. "But she's looking. And here's what worries me: the moment Steve wakes up and tells you where it is, the moment you start moving toward Chicago or wherever, her people could spot you, could follow you, could get there first."

"And destroy the evidence."

"Or worse. Set a trap. Wait for you to show up. Handle all her problems at once."

I sat back, the weight of it pressing down. "So what do we do?"

"You wait for Steve to wake up. You get the location from him. And then you move fast. Faster than Margaret's people can react. You get that evidence, and you get it to the FBI before she can destroy it." Noreen paused. "But you need to understand that once Steve tells anyone where it is, the clock starts. Margaret has people everywhere: phone taps, surveillance, informants. The window is small."

"How small?"

"Hours. Maybe less. From the moment Steve reveals the location to the moment Margaret's people get there. That's your window." She hung up.

I looked at Griffin. "Margaret doesn't know where the evidence is yet, but she's looking. And the moment Steve tells us—"

"She could find out, follow us, get there first." Griffin ran his hand through his hair. "This is worse than I thought."

I thought about Steve in surgery, unconscious, unable to tell us anything. I thought about Margaret's people already narrowing down locations, already watching, already waiting. I thought about Roth meeting with her lawyers tomorrow at 2 PM. Less than 24 hours. "We need Steve to wake up," I said. "We need him conscious and coherent. Soon."

"Surgery should be done in about three hours, then recovery after that. He might be conscious by tonight."

"And then?"

"Then we find out where this evidence is, and we get there before Margaret does."

At 2:51 PM, the surgeon came out. "He's stable. We removed the infected tissue, cleaned the wound, and started strong IV antibiotics. He'll need at least 48 hours before he's strong enough to move, but he should make a full recovery."

"When can I see him?"

"He's in recovery, still sedated. But you can see him briefly."

She led me to recovery. Steve was on a bed, tubes everywhere, monitors beeping, but breathing, alive. I sat next to him and waited. His eyes flickered, opened slightly. "Olivia?"

"I'm here. You're okay. Surgery went well."

"How long... was I out?"

"About three hours. It's almost 3 PM."

His eyes widened. Fear. "Need to... tell you... evidence..."

"Not yet. Rest first. You just had surgery."

"No. Listen." He grabbed my wrist. Weak but urgent. "Margaret... she's looking for it. Doesn't know where yet. But she's smart. She'll figure it out."

"Where is it?"

"Chicago. Bank of America. Madison Street branch. Safe deposit box 2847." He fumbled in his hospital gown. "Key... where are my clothes?"

"In the closet. Why?"

"The key's in my wallet. Hidden compartment. You need to—" He stopped. Eyes closing. Too weak to continue.

"Steve?"

"Get it... before she does..." His voice faded. "Before she destroys it..." He passed out.

The nurse touched my shoulder. "He needs rest. The sedation is still in his system. Come back in a few hours."

I went back to the family room. Griffin was there. "He woke up. Told me where the evidence is."

"Where?"

"Chicago. Bank of America. Madison Street. Box 2847. He has the key."

"Then we go. Tonight."

"He also said Margaret's looking for it. That she doesn't know where yet but she's trying to figure it out."

Griffin pulled out his phone. "Let me make some calls. See if we can get ahead of this." He walked away, starting to talk quietly.

I sat there, thinking. Margaret looking but not knowing. Yet. Evidence in Chicago. Four hours away. Roth meeting with Margaret's lawyers tomorrow at 2 PM. The window was closing.

Griffin came back. His face was grim. "I just talked to my supervisor. We have a problem."

"What problem?"

"Hospital administrator called me. Someone contacted them twenty minutes ago. Asked if Steve Adler was a patient here. Used his real name."

My stomach dropped. "What did they say?"

"Hospital policy can't confirm or deny. But whoever called knew he was here. Knew his real name. That means Margaret's people are already tracking him."

"How?"

"Could be anything. They spotted the ambulance. License plate. Someone saw us entering the hospital. Maybe they're calling every hospital in Cleveland asking about him." Griffin sat down. "Point is, they know he's here. They just don't know what floor. What room."

"Does that matter?"

"It matters because they're getting closer. And here's what worries me more. If they know he's here, they know he'll eventually tell us where the evidence is. They're probably already moving on likely locations."

"You think they're going to Chicago?"

"I think they're covering their bases. Margaret's smart. She knows Steve would hide evidence somewhere accessible. A major city within driving distance. Chicago is obvious. So is Pittsburgh. Detroit. Maybe Cincinnati." He pulled up a map on his phone. "She probably has people watching storage facilities, banks, anywhere someone might hide documents in all these cities."

"But she doesn't know which specific bank. Which box."

"Not yet. But she will. The moment we move toward Chicago, the moment we show up at that bank, her people could be watching. They could follow us. They could see where we go."

"So what do we do?"

"We move tonight. While Steve's still unconscious. While Margaret's people think we can't act yet. We get there, get the evidence, and get out before they realize what's happening."

"Steve said he needs to be there."

"Can't risk it. He's too weak. And if we wait for him to recover, Margaret's people will have more time to narrow down the location. They might even find it first."

"He has the key. It's in his wallet."

"Then we take his wallet. We go tonight. Before Margaret figures out exactly where to look."

"Okay. Tonight. But we need to be careful. If Margaret's people spot us—"

"They won't. We'll take back roads. Unmarked car. We go dark. Get there. Get the evidence. Get back before anyone knows we left."

"And Steve?"

"Stays here. Protected. We leave agents with him. If Margaret's people find this room, they find a post-surgical patient with no information and a dozen FBI agents."

The plan made sense. But it felt wrong leaving Steve behind. "He wanted to be there," I said.

"He wanted the evidence secured. That's what matters." Griffin stood up. "I'll arrange the transport. Secure vehicle."

He walked away to make arrangements. I sat there, looking at the clock. Six hours until we left. The window was open. But it was closing fast.

"How many agents can you get here to protect Steve?"

"Twelve by 5 PM. Enough to secure this floor completely. No one gets near Steve's room without federal ID."

"And Chicago?"

"Four-hour drive. We leave at 8 PM and arrive at midnight. The bank won't be open, but we can case it. Make sure Margaret's people aren't already there. Hit it first thing in the morning when it opens."

"That's too long. Roth meets with Margaret's lawyers at 2 PM tomorrow. We need the evidence back here by then."

"Banks open at 9 AM. We get the evidence at 9. Four hours back. We're here by 1 PM. That's an hour before Roth's meeting."

"Cutting it close."

"It's the only option we have," Griffin said.

By 5:13 PM, the FBI agents arrived. Twelve of them took positions in the hallway, at the elevators, and at the stairwell doors. Griffin set up a command post at the nurses' station, with monitors showing security cameras, every entrance, and every exit. "We're locked down. Steve's secure. No one gets to him without going through us."

"And if Margaret's people try?"

"We arrest them. But I don't think they will. Not yet. They're still trying to figure out where the evidence is. They don't know Steve already told us."

I went to Steve's room. He was still unconscious, monitors beeping steadily. I found his clothes in the closet and located his wallet. Hidden compartment inside. Small key. Box 2847. I put the key in my pocket.

"I'm going to get your evidence," I whispered. "I promise I'll bring it back." He didn't respond. Just kept breathing. Steady. Alive.

I called Linda. "I'm leaving the hospital tonight. Going to Chicago to get the evidence."

"Is that safe?"

"No. But it's necessary. Margaret's people are looking for it. We need to get there first."

"What about Steve?"

"He stays here. FBI protection. He'll be safe."

"And you?"

"I'll be back by tomorrow afternoon. Before Roth's meeting."

"Be careful."

"I will. Kiss Grace for me."

"I will." I hung up.

Griffin came in. "Vehicle's ready. Unmarked SUV. Full tank. We leave in two hours."

"Why wait?"

"Darkness. We don't want to be seen leaving. Less traffic at night. Easier to spot if we're being followed."

That made sense. "What about the bank? Do they know we're coming?"

"I called the FBI field office in Chicago. They'll have agents at the bank when it opens. Secure perimeter. If Margaret's people are watching, we'll spot them."

"And if they're already inside the bank?"

"Then we deal with it. But my gut says she doesn't know which bank yet. She's probably covering multiple locations, spreading her resources thin. That gives us an advantage." I hoped he was right.

At 7:47 PM, Steve woke up briefly. I was sitting in his room, waiting. His eyes opened. "Olivia?"

"I'm here."

"Did you... tell them... where it is?"

"Yes. We're going tonight. To Chicago. We'll get it."

"I should... come with you..."

"You just had surgery. You need to rest."

"If Margaret's people... are there..."

"We'll handle it. The FBI is coming with us. We'll be protected."

He closed his eyes. "Be careful. She's... dangerous. More dangerous... than you know..."

"I know."

He relaxed. "Thank you... for this. For everything."

"Save your thanks. We haven't gotten it yet."

He smiled weakly. "But you will. I believe... you will." He fell back asleep.

At 8:03 PM, Griffin appeared at the door. "Time to go." I stood and looked at Steve one more time. Sleeping. Protected. Safe. We left the room, walked past FBI agents, down the service elevator, and out the back entrance. An unmarked SUV was waiting. Dark blue. Nothing special. Could be anyone's car.

Another agent was in the driver's seat. Young. Maybe thirty. "Special Agent Torres. I'll be driving tonight." We got in. The doors closed. Torres pulled away. No rush. Just normal traffic.

"We're going dark in five minutes," Griffin said. "Phones off. No communication until we're back in Cleveland." I turned off my phone. Griffin did the same.

We drove through Cleveland, past the city lights, onto the highway heading west, toward Chicago. Toward the evidence.

The car was quiet. Just the hum of the engine. The road stretched ahead in the darkness.

Torres took back roads once we left the city, avoiding toll booths, avoiding cameras, avoiding anything that could track us. Griffin was watching behind us, making sure no one was following. "Clear so far."

"How long?" I asked.

"Three and a half hours if traffic is good. Should arrive around 11:30 PM."

"Then what?"

"We find a hotel near the bank, get a few hours of sleep, and be at the bank when it opens at 9 AM." He looked at me. "You should rest. It's going to be a long night."

But I couldn't rest. I sat in the back seat, staring out the window, watching the darkness blur past, thinking about Steve in the hospital, Margaret somewhere searching, and Roth meeting with her lawyers tomorrow. I thought about how close we were to losing everything. Everything was on the line. The miles rolled by. Past farms. Past small towns, past darkness and silence.

At 11:34 PM, the Chicago skyline appeared, lights against darkness. Torres drove to the financial district and found the

Bank of America on Madison Street. Dark, closed, quiet. "There it is," Griffin said.

We circled the block, looking for surveillance, watchers, or any sign of Margaret's people. Nothing obvious.

He found a hotel two blocks away. Small, cheap, the kind of place that doesn't ask questions. We checked in. Two rooms. Cash. No IDs.

"Get some sleep," Griffin said. "We move at 8:30 AM. The bank opens at 9. We're in and out in fifteen minutes."

"And if Margaret's people are there?"

"Then we adapt. But we're FBI. We're armed. We're trained. They're private security at best. We have the advantage."

I hoped he was right. I went to my room, lay on the bed, and stared at the ceiling. I couldn't sleep. Tomorrow morning we'd either get the evidence or walk into a trap. I closed my eyes, tried to rest, but all I could think about was that safe deposit box. Evidence that could destroy Margaret or evidence that her people had already destroyed. We wouldn't know until morning, until we opened that box and saw what was inside.

Chapter Four

The Locked Box

I DIDN'T SLEEP. I lay in the hotel bed staring at the ceiling, listening to sirens outside. Chicago never sleeps. Never stops. Neither could I. My mind kept spinning through scenarios: what we'd find in that box, what we wouldn't, whether Margaret's people were already in that bank, waiting.

At 6:47 AM, my phone buzzed. Griffin: *Torres checked perimeter. Clear. Meet lobby 8:30.*

I got up, showered, and tried to eat the stale bagel from the hotel breakfast. I took one bite and threw it away.

At 8:27 AM, I went downstairs. Griffin was already there, Torres next to him, both in dark suits. They could be lawyers, businessmen, or anyone. That was the point.

"Sleep?" Griffin asked.

"No."

"Me neither." He handed me coffee. I didn't drink it. "Torres walked the block three times. No surveillance he could spot."

Griffin checked his watch. "We go in at nine exactly. Get the box. Fifteen minutes maximum. If anything feels wrong, we abort."

"And if Margaret's people are inside?"

"Then we adapt."

We walked two blocks through early morning Chicago. People were heading to work, coffee shops were opening, taxis were honking. Normal. We weren't normal.

The Bank of America building rose ahead, forty stories of glass and steel. The morning sun reflected off the windows like fire.

"Cameras everywhere," Torres muttered. "If Margaret's monitoring security feeds—"

"She'll know we're here within minutes," Griffin finished. "Can't be helped." My chest was tight; it was hard to breathe.

At 8:58 AM, employees started arriving. A woman in a blue uniform unlocked the front doors. At 8:59 AM, she turned the sign to OPEN.

"Now," Griffin said. We crossed the street, through revolving doors, into the lobby. Cold air hit me. Marble floors, high ceilings, everything echoing. A receptionist looked up, twenty-something, with perfect makeup and a professional smile. "Good morning. How can I—"

Griffin pulled out his badge and showed it quickly, not letting her study it. "FBI. We need access to a safe deposit box."

Her smile disappeared. "I'll need to get my manager."

"Please do that."

She picked up the phone and spoke quietly. I couldn't hear what she said. She hung up. "He'll be right with you."

We waited, standing in that lobby, visible to anyone watching. I looked at the windows, at the people walking past outside, at the security cameras in the corners. Any of them could be Margaret's. Every second felt like an hour.

A man emerged from the back, in his fifties, wearing a gray suit, with nervous energy in his movements. "I'm Robert, branch manager." He looked at Griffin's badge, really looked this time. "You're FBI?"

"Special Agent Griffin. This is Special Agent Torres, and Ms. Parker." Griffin pulled out papers. "We need access to safe deposit box 2847."

"Do you have a warrant?"

"We have the key. The box belongs to a federal witness under our protection. These documents authorize access."

Robert took the papers. He read them slowly. Too slowly. I watched the front entrance, looking for anyone watching us. A businessman walked past, glanced in, and kept walking. A woman with a briefcase entered and went to a teller. Normal. Everything looked normal. That's what scared me.

"These appear to be in order," Robert finally said. "But I'll need to verify—"

"We don't have time for verification," Griffin said. His voice was calm but firm. "That box contains evidence in an active federal investigation. Every minute we wait increases the risk of compromise."

Robert's face tightened. "I still need to follow protocol—"

"Make a call. Verify the badge number. But do it while we're accessing the box." Griffin wasn't asking. "This is a time-sensitive operation."

Robert looked between us, calculating. "Follow me."

He led us through the lobby, past tellers, and through a door marked "Authorized Personnel Only." He swiped his card. The lock clicked. The door opened into a narrow hallway with fluorescent lights and no windows. Another door was ahead. Another swipe. Another lock. The safe deposit box room. Cold. Silent. Walls lined with small metal doors. Hundreds of them, all identical except for numbers.

"Box 2847 is on the far wall."

Robert walked. We followed. The room felt too quiet, like a tomb. He found the number: 2847. Small brass plate. Unremarkable. "I'll need the key."

I pulled it from my pocket. Robert took it, inserted it into the top lock, and turned it. Then he used his master key on the bottom lock and turned that. The door opened. Inside was a metal box. Long. Maybe eighteen inches. Narrow. Heavy-looking.

Robert pulled it out, grunted slightly. It was heavy. "The privacy room is through here."

He carried the box and led us to a small room with a table, two chairs, and no security cameras.

"Take your time." He set the box on the table. "I'll be at my desk if you need anything." He left and closed the door.

The three of us stared at that box. Everything we'd fought for. Everything we needed. Maybe everything that could destroy Margaret. Inside a locked metal box.

"Small combination lock," Torres said. "Four digits."

"Steve didn't mention a combination," I said.

Griffin examined it. Standard lock. Could buy it at any hardware store. "Try the box number: 2-8-4-7."

Torres turned the dial. 2. 8. 4. 7. Click. The lock opened. "That's either very clever or very stupid," Torres muttered.

Griffin lifted the lid. Inside were USB drives. Six of them. Black. Each labeled with a white marker. 2013. 2014. 2015. 2016. 2017. 2018.

Six years, condensed into six pieces of plastic. Below the drives were papers. Documents. I pulled them out: bank statements. Dozens of them. Transfers highlighted in yellow. Amounts circled. Dates marked. Transfer authorizations. Margaret's signature at the bottom of each one. Photos. Surveillance photos. Margaret meeting with men outside nightclubs, in parking lots. Men in leather jackets. Gang colors visible.

"This is good," Griffin said quietly. "This is very good."

Torres pulled out his laptop and opened it. "Let me check the drives. Make sure they're readable."

He plugged in the 2013 drive. The laptop made a sound. A window opened. PASSWORD REQUIRED. My stomach dropped. "It's encrypted," Torres said.

"What?"

"Password protected. We can't access it without the password." He unplugged it and tried the 2014 drive.

Same window. PASSWORD REQUIRED. He tried all six drives, one by one. All encrypted. All locked.

"Steve password-protected everything," Torres said. His voice was flat. "We can't access any of these files without the passwords."

"He didn't tell me about passwords."

"Maybe he forgot to mention it. Maybe he assumed we'd know." Griffin pulled out his phone. "I'll call the hospital. Get Steve on the phone. He can tell us."

He dialed and put it on speaker. Three rings. Four. Five. "Metro Hospital, sixth-floor nurses' station."

"This is Special Agent Griffin. I need to speak with Steve Adler in room 6-17. It's urgent."

"I'm sorry, Mr. Adler's condition deteriorated overnight. His fever spiked again, and he's heavily sedated. Doctor's orders."

Griffin's jaw tightened. "When will he wake up?"

"The doctor said possibly this afternoon. But his infection is fighting the antibiotics. It could be hours. Could be longer."

"We need him conscious now. This is a federal investigation. Can you reduce the sedation?"

"Sir, he's septic. We had to increase his medication to keep him stable. Reducing it now could be dangerous. We can't risk his recovery."

"How long until—"

"I don't know. I'm sorry. The doctor will update you when there's any change."

Griffin hung up. "Fuck."

Torres was still staring at the drives. "We could try brute forcing the encryption. But these look like 256-bit. It could take months to crack. Maybe years."

"We don't have years. We don't have months." Griffin checked his watch. "Roth's meeting with Margaret's lawyers is at 2 PM today. That's—" he calculated "—four hours and twenty-three minutes."

"Can we stop the meeting?" I asked. "Show Roth these documents? Even without the drives?"

"Bank statements and transfer authorizations?" Griffin scanned them. "Margaret's signature on financial documents. But they don't prove what the money was for. Her lawyers will say legitimate business expenses, vendor payments, legal transactions."

"What about the surveillance photos?"

"Margaret meeting with people. Doesn't prove criminal activity. Could be anything." He looked at the USB drives. "The real evidence is on these. Steve said there were emails, communications, security camera footage from Club Vertical. That's what proves intent. That's what proves she knew she was laundering money."

"So without the passwords—"

"Without the passwords, we have circumstantial evidence that proves nothing."

The room felt smaller. Colder. Torres was examining the papers more closely. "Wait. There's something here."

He held up a document. Handwritten notes. Steve's handwriting. Numbers. Letters. Random characters. "These could be password hints," Torres said.

Griffin looked. "Try them."

Torres typed the first sequence into the 2013 drive. INCORRECT PASSWORD. 2 ATTEMPTS REMAINING. "Stop," Griffin said. "Two wrong and the drive locks permanently. All data erased."

"Then we can't guess," I said. "We need Steve."

"Steve's unconscious."

"Then we wait for him to wake up."

"We don't have time to wait." Griffin was pacing now. Small room. Only a few steps. "Roth is meeting Margaret's lawyers in four hours. If he signs that settlement, if Titan walks away, Margaret wins. The proxy fight is over. She keeps the company. She keeps her power."

"And the criminal investigation?"

"Continues. But without institutional backing from Titan Capital, without their forensic accountants and lawyers helping build the case, it's much weaker. Prosecutors look at cases they can win. This becomes harder to win."

A knock on the door. We all froze. Robert opened it. His face was pale. "I'm sorry to interrupt. But there are two men outside asking about you."

My blood went cold. "Who are they?"

"They said they're private investigators. Said they're looking for a woman with two men in suits who might have entered the bank this morning."

Griffin and Torres exchanged looks. "They saw us," Torres said quietly.

"How?"

"Followed us from Cleveland. Staked out the hotel. Doesn't matter." Griffin started packing the drives and documents into his bag. "We need to leave. Now."

"What about the passwords?"

"We take everything. Figure it out later." He zipped the bag. "Robert, is there another exit?"

"Service entrance. Through the back. Leads to the parking garage."

"Show us. Quickly."

Robert led us out. Down a different hallway. Past offices. To a metal door with a push bar. "Through here. Down one flight. Garage exit is on Monroe Street."

"Thank you," Griffin said.

We pushed through the door. Into a concrete stairwell. Started running down. Our footsteps echoed. Too loud. Too obvious. Metal door at the bottom. Griffin pushed it open. Parking garage. Dark. Smelled like gasoline and exhaust. Cars everywhere.

"Where's our vehicle?" I asked.

"Roosevelt Street. Two blocks north." Griffin looked around. "We go on foot. Stay in groups of people. Look normal."

We moved. Between parked cars. Toward the exit ramp. The morning sun was bright after the darkness. Made me squint. We walked. Fast but not running. Just people late for work. Just normal. I kept looking behind us. Couldn't help it. No one following. Not yet.

One block. Two blocks. Our SUV appeared. Black. Unmarked. Torres's excellent parallel parking job. "Get in," Griffin said. Keys already out.

We jumped in. Doors slamming. Griffin started the engine. Pulled into traffic. "Check behind us," he said.

I turned. Looked through the back window. Traffic. Taxis. Delivery trucks. Normal Chicago morning. Then I saw it. Black sedan. Tinted windows. Three cars back.

"There," I said. "Black sedan."

Torres pulled out binoculars. Looked. "Two men. Driver and passenger. Both watching us."

"Are they following or just driving?"

Torres watched for three blocks. "Following. They're staying back but matching our speed. Every turn we make, they make."

"Professional tail," Griffin said. "They're not trying to hide anymore. They know we spotted them."

"What do they want?"

"To see where we go. Where Steve is. Where the evidence ends up." Griffin turned. Side street. Less traffic. "We lose them, then head back to Cleveland. Can't lead them to the hospital."

Twenty minutes of turns. Alleys. One-way streets. Chicago maze. The sedan kept appearing. Different distances. Different angles. But always there. "Can't shake them," Torres said. "They're too good."

Griffin pulled into an underground garage. Drove to the lowest level. Parked behind a concrete pillar. Killed the engine. We waited. Silent. Barely breathing. Two minutes. Three. The sedan didn't appear. "Lost them," Torres whispered.

"Or they're waiting at the exit," Griffin said.

My phone rang. Made me jump. The sound was too loud in the quiet garage. Noreen. I answered. "Hello?"

"Where are you?" Her voice was sharp. Stressed. "Did you get the evidence?"

"We got it. But there's a problem."

"What problem?"

"The USB drives are encrypted. Password protected. We can't access any of the files. And Steve's still unconscious at the hospital."

Silence. Long silence. Then: "You're telling me you have the evidence but you can't use it."

"Yes."

"And Roth's meeting is in—" I heard her checking "—three hours and forty-seven minutes."

"I know."

"Then it's over." Her voice cracked. "Without evidence, Roth is going to sign. He's going to take Margaret's settlement."

"We'll get Steve to wake up. We'll get the passwords—"

"When? This afternoon? Tonight? Tomorrow? Roth is meeting Margaret's lawyers at 2 PM. Not tonight. Not tomorrow. Today." She was crying now. Trying to hide it. Failing. "We lost."

"Noreen—"

"I have to go. I have to be in that meeting. I have to watch Roth sign away everything my father died for. Because of passwords nobody can remember." She hung up.

I looked at Griffin. At Torres. At the bag containing encrypted drives we couldn't open. "Roth is signing at 2 PM," I said. "We can't stop it."

Griffin hit the steering wheel. Once. Hard. "There has to be a way."

"What way? We don't have the passwords. Steve's unconscious. We're sitting in a parking garage hiding from Margaret's people. What exactly can we do?"

"We could go to Roth directly," Torres suggested. "Show him what we have. The documents. The photos. Maybe it's enough to make him pause."

"It's not enough." Griffin was staring at the bag. "He'll say it's circumstantial. His lawyers will say the same thing. Without the emails and communications that prove intent, this is just paper."

"So we're giving up?"

"We're being realistic." Griffin started the engine. "We get back to Cleveland. We wait for Steve to wake up. We get the passwords. And then we take everything to federal prosecutors. Build a criminal case. It takes longer but—"

My phone rang again. Different number. Cleveland area code. I answered. "Hello?"

"Ms. Parker? This is Dr. Williams. Metro Hospital."

My heart stopped. "Is Steve—"

"Mr. Adler is still unconscious. But I'm calling because we just received some unusual requests regarding his care."

"What kind of requests?"

"Two different people called within the last hour. Both claiming to be family members. Both asking very specific questions about his condition. His room number. When he might wake up. Whether he can have visitors."

Margaret's people. Already. "What did you tell them?"

"Hospital policy prohibits us from confirming or denying patient information. But I wanted to alert you because the calls felt... coordinated. Like they were trying to get information from different angles."

"Thank you. We're on our way back now. Can you increase security on his room?"

"We already have FBI agents stationed there. But I'll notify them about the calls." She hung up.

"Margaret's people are calling the hospital," I told Griffin. "Trying to find out about Steve."

"They probably followed us from Cleveland. Watched us go into the bank. Now they're trying to figure out what we found." Griffin pulled out of the garage. Different exit. Residential street. "We need to get back. Make sure Steve's protected."

We got on the highway. Heading east. Toward Cleveland. Nobody spoke for twenty miles. The silence was suffocating.

At 11:34 AM, my phone buzzed. Text from Noreen: *Roth moved the meeting up. 1 PM instead of 2. Margaret wants to close this fast.*

I showed Griffin. "That's one hour and twenty-six minutes from now. We're still ninety minutes from Cleveland."

"So we can't make it even if we wanted to."

"Even if we had the passwords. Even if we could show him everything." Griffin pushed the speedometer higher. "It's over." We drove.

At 12:47 PM, another text from Noreen. *Margaret's lawyers just arrived. Three of them. They brought the settlement papers. Roth is reviewing them now.*

I read it twice. Won. Margaret won. Despite everything. Despite Steve's evidence. She won. Because of passwords. Because life isn't fair and justice isn't guaranteed, and sometimes you do everything right and still lose.

At 1:03 PM, final text. Noreen: *He's signing.* That was it. Two words. *He's signing.* I stared at those words until they blurred.

Griffin's phone rang. He answered. Listened. His face changed. "When?" Pause. "How long do we have?" Longer pause. "We're twenty minutes out."

He hung up. Looked at me. "That was my supervisor. SEC just issued an emergency order. They're putting a temporary hold on the Titan Capital settlement."

My heart jumped. "What?"

"SEC is investigating whether Margaret disclosed material information to Titan during settlement negotiations. If she lied or withheld information about the criminal investigation, the settlement could be voided."

"When did this happen?"

"Ten minutes ago. Right as Roth was about to sign." Griffin was driving faster now, weaving through traffic. "Apparently, someone tipped off the SEC. Sent them a package of documents showing Margaret knew about the money laundering investigation weeks ago but didn't disclose it to Titan."

"Who sent it?"

"Anonymous. But the timing is perfect. The settlement is on hold for 72 hours while the SEC investigates."

"So we have three days."

"We have three days to get those passwords, to access the encrypted drives, to show Roth and the SEC exactly what Margaret's been hiding." Griffin looked at me. "This is our window. Our only chance."

"Steve's still unconscious."

"Then he better wake up soon. Because if he doesn't, if we can't access that evidence in 72 hours, the SEC lifts the hold. Roth signs the settlement. And Margaret walks."

We pulled off the highway, Cleveland exits, getting close. "Hospital is ten minutes away," Torres said.

My phone buzzed. Text from the doctor. *Steve just woke up.* I showed Griffin. He pushed the accelerator to the floor. "Hold on." We raced through Cleveland streets, red lights, traffic. It didn't matter.

The hospital appeared. Griffin pulled into the emergency bay. Illegal parking. Didn't care. We ran inside, to the elevators, up to the sixth floor, down the hallway, past FBI agents, to Steve's room. The door was open. Steve was sitting up, color better than yesterday, eyes clear. Tubes and wires still everywhere, but awake, conscious, alive.

"Olivia." His voice was hoarse but steady. "Did you get it?"

"We got it." I pulled the bag forward. "But there's a problem."

His face fell. "What problem?"

"The drives are encrypted. All six of them. We need the passwords."

Steve looked at the bag, at the six black USB drives inside. "Of course they are," he said quietly. "I always encrypt sensitive files."

"Do you remember the passwords?"

He closed his eyes, thinking. "Yes. Yes, I remember them."

Relief flooded through me so fast I nearly collapsed. "Can you write them down?"

"No. Too risky. Someone could find them." He opened his eyes. "But I can unlock the drives myself. How long do we have?"

"72 hours. The SEC put a temporary hold on Margaret's settlement. But after 72 hours, the hold lifts. Roth signs. It's over."

"Then we need to move fast." Steve tried to sit up further, winced. "Get me a laptop. I'll start unlocking files now."

Griffin was already pulling one out, Torres connecting it, setting it up on the rolling table. Steve took the first USB drive, 2013, plugged it in. The password prompt appeared. His fingers moved across the keyboard, fast, certain. The drive unlocked. Files appeared. Hundreds of them: emails, bank records, communications.

"That's one," Steve said. "Five more to go." He plugged in the 2014 drive, typed another password, and unlocked it. More files. More evidence. Years of Margaret's crimes. All six drives open. All the evidence accessible. Six years of documentation. Everything Margaret did. Everyone she paid. Every crime she committed. Right there on the laptop screen.

Steve looked at me, exhausted but determined. "Now," he said. "Now we take her down."

Chapter Five

What the Video Showed

STEVE'S FINGERS MOVED ACROSS the keyboard. Files appeared on the screen. Hundreds of them. Six years of Margaret's crimes organized in folders.

My hands wouldn't stop shaking. "How much is here?" My voice came out wrong.

Steve scrolled through folder after folder. "Everything."

I just stood there. This was it. This was the answer I'd been chasing for seven years. Somewhere in these files was the reason Leo died.

"Where do we start?" Torres asked.

"2014." The word came out too loud. Everyone looked at me.

"Leo died in 2014," I said.

Steve's expression changed, something like pity. "Are you sure—"

"Yes."

He opened the 2014 folder. Then April 2014. More folders inside: emails, bank records, security footage.

"Fifth Street," I said. "Club Vertical. Anything that connects Margaret to Leo."

Steve opened the Security Footage - CV Millfield folder. Videos were organized by date, from April 1st through April 30th. He scrolled. April 14. April 15. April 16. He stopped at April 14. The file name read: CV_BackAlley_041414_2330.mp4. "Four days before Leo died," Torres said quietly.

Steve clicked it. Black-and-white footage from a security camera. Timestamp: April 14, 2014, 11:47 PM.

The scene showed the back alley of Club Vertical. Dumpsters. Loading dock. Empty, except... Steve pointed. "There." A shadow by the dumpster. Someone sitting against the wall.

He zoomed in. Thin. Hunched. Hoodie too big. The room tilted. That hoodie. I bought that hoodie at Goodwill for Leo's seventeenth birthday. He wore it every day. They buried him in it because it was the only thing he owned that was whole.

"That's him," I whispered. "That's Leo."

On screen, Leo sat with his head down. Probably sleeping. He slept there sometimes, behind the dumpster where it was warmer.

The timestamp moved: 11:48. 11:49. 11:50. Nothing happened. Then headlights swept the alley. A car pulled in. A black sedan. Two men got out. Big. Moving fast. They opened the back door and dragged someone out. A young man, early twenties. Hands tied behind his back. Duct tape over his mouth. Fighting. Trying to twist away.

"Don't—" I started.

Steve didn't stop the video. The men forced the victim to his knees, right there in the alley, ten feet from where Leo slept. One held him while the other pulled out a gun. Long barrel. Suppressor attached.

My stomach turned. The gun went to the victim's head, the back of the skull. The victim shook, trying to scream through the tape. The gun flashed. No sound, just light. The victim's head snapped forward. Body went limp. Fell. Blood spread.

I couldn't look away. Couldn't move. Couldn't breathe. Behind the dumpster, Leo jerked awake, his whole body flinching. The killers were checking the body, making sure he was dead.

Leo stared at them, at the blood, at the gun. Then he moved, trying to stand quietly. His foot hit something. A bottle. It rolled, clinking against the dumpster. Both killers turned, looking right at Leo. Nobody moved. Three seconds that felt like forever. Then Leo ran.

One killer started after him, but the other grabbed his arm and pointed at the body, at the mess. They let Leo go, but they watched, getting a good look at his face, his hoodie, everything.

One pulled out a phone and started typing. The video kept playing. They loaded the body into their trunk, cleaned the blood, and threw rags in the dumpster. Then they just stood there, smoking and waiting.

At 12:03 AM, another car pulled in. A black Mercedes. Margaret's car. She got out, looking perfect at midnight in a business suit, hair pulled back. She walked over as if this was normal. They talked. No audio, but I watched them point at the trunk, at where Leo had been.

Margaret walked to the trunk. One killer opened it. She looked inside. Her face didn't change at all. She nodded and handed something to the killer. Money probably. They talked for a few more minutes, then she got in her car and drove away. The killers closed the trunk and left.

The alley was empty, as if nothing had happened. The video ended. I couldn't move. "He saw them," my voice came out broken. "Leo saw them kill someone."

"Yes," Steve said.

"And Margaret came after, to check, to pay them."

"Yes."

Griffin came back. "There's audio from April 15th, two hours after this."

Steve pulled it up and hit play. Static. Then Margaret's voice, cold and controlled.

"We have a problem."

A male voice, deep. "What kind?"

"Someone saw the Henderson matter last night."

"Who?"

"A homeless man, a Fifth Street regular, sleeping behind the dumpster. He woke up during the execution."

Pause. "How much did he see?"

"Everything. Victor said he was right there, watched it, then made noise trying to leave. They got a good look."

"And?"

"And I arrived sixteen minutes later. He could have still been watching, could have seen me at the scene, seen me check the body."

Longer pause. "Want me to handle it?"

The pause felt like forever. Then Margaret said, "He's a witness to murder. He can place me at a homicide scene."

"I understand."

"I don't want him found talking to the police. I don't want him found at all. Ever."

"I understand."

"Make it clean. Make it look like his own business. Drug debt. Gang dispute. Nothing that connects to Henderson, nothing to the club, nothing to me."

"When?"

"Soon. Before he talks, before he runs, before anyone knows." Her voice got harder. "Find him, watch him. When you can, eliminate him."

"Consider it done."

"This can't come back to me."

"It won't. The witness will be handled."

The recording ended. Complete silence. I couldn't feel my hands, couldn't feel anything. "She ordered it." Each word hurt to say. "Margaret ordered them to kill Leo."

"Yes," Torres said.

"Because he saw her at a murder scene."

"Yes."

My legs gave out. I sat down hard. The room was spinning, and my vision was going dark at the edges.

This was my fault. If I'd answered his calls. If I'd given him money. If I'd just picked up the phone. But no. That's not right. Even if I'd answered. Even if I'd paid. Margaret still would have killed him. Because he saw.

"Who was Henderson?" My voice cracked.

Steve pulled up a report. "Marcus Henderson. Twenty-three. Low-level dealer. He was skimming from Margaret's gang, the one she used for money laundering. Went missing April 14th. Body never found."

"So Margaret ordered Henderson killed. Leo witnessed it. Then Margaret ordered Leo killed."

"Yes."

I thought about the police. Detective Doyle. Sitting across from me. Telling me Leo died over drug debt. Eight thousand dollars. Telling me Leo had my number in his pocket. That he kept saying, "Livvy will save me."

And I'd believed it. For seven years, I believed Leo died because I didn't save him. Because I chose my thesis over his life. But that's not what happened.

Leo died because he was in the wrong place. Because a bottle rolled. Because Margaret Carrington wanted no witnesses.

"How long?" I asked. "Between that call and when they killed him?"

Steve checked. "Recording was April 15th at 2:13 AM. Leo died April 18th around midnight."

"Three days." My voice was barely there. "They hunted him for three days."

Torres pulled up text messages. "Between the gang leader and another member."

He showed me.

April 15, 2:47 PM: *Found him. Fifth Street homeless camp. Same guy from Monday.*

April 16, 8:33 AM: *He's moving around. Sleeping in different spots. Knows something's wrong.*

April 16, 11:41 PM: *Lost him. Smart. Staying in crowds. Never alone.*

April 17, 3:15 PM: *Still tracking. He'll slip up.*

April 17, 11:52 PM: *Got him. Alone behind warehouse on Fifth. Moving in.*

April 18, 12:09 AM: *It's done. Clean. Same as Henderson. On his knees. Back of head.*

"They hunted him." My voice didn't sound like mine. It felt like someone else was speaking through me.

"For three days they hunted my brother like an animal."

Steve pulled up crime scene photos. I grabbed the laptop before he could stop me. Leo. Face down. Blood everywhere. Gunshot wound to the back of the head.

I had to look away. Medical examiner's report. Time of death: April 18, 12:17 AM. Leo died at 12:17 AM. I was in my dorm, probably asleep or studying, deleting his texts without reading them while he was on his knees behind a warehouse, gun to his head, calling for me.

"There's more," Steve said quietly. "Financial record. April 19th." Transfer authorization. Margaret's signature. **To:** Victor Holdings LLC, **Amount:** $100,000, **Date:** April 19, 2014. The day after Leo's body was found.

"She paid them one hundred thousand dollars." My voice was shaking now. "For killing my brother."

"For both," Griffin said. "Henderson and Leo."

Fifty thousand dollars. That's what Leo's life was worth. I stood up. I had to move. I had to get out. "Olivia—" Griffin started. I walked out. Down the hospital hallway. Found the stairs. Kept going.

Outside, the air was cold. I couldn't feel it. All I could see was Leo. Running. Hiding. Knowing they were coming. Did he try to call me? Those last three days? I'd deleted his texts and sent calls to voicemail. Because I was busy. Because my thesis mattered. Because I thought tough love would help. And Leo was being hunted.

I sank down right there on the sidewalk and put my head in my hands. Detective Doyle's voice echoed in my mind. *He kept saying 'Livvy will save me.' right up until the end.*

Leo died believing I'd come. But I didn't come. And now I knew. Even if I had come, even if I'd answered every call, even if I'd given him every penny, it wouldn't have mattered. Margaret wanted him dead. So he died.

The door opened behind me. Griffin came out. "We have enough," he said. "Video. Audio. Texts. Financial records. This is first-degree murder. Margaret's looking at life in prison."

"When?"

"I'm calling the U.S. Attorney now. Emergency meeting today."

He made the call, talked for a few minutes, then hung up. "Two hours. They'll see us in two hours."

"I need to call Linda." I pulled out my phone and stared at it. How do I tell her? How do I say the words? I called.

Linda answered quickly. "How's it going?"

"We found it." My voice came out shaky. "Linda, we found what happened to Leo."

Silence. Then: "What do you mean?"

"The evidence. Steve had everything. Video. Audio. Records." I couldn't stop my hands from trembling. "We know how Leo died. We know why."

"Tell me." Her voice grew quiet, the way it did when she was bracing for something bad. "Tell me everything."

I took a breath and explained everything. All of it.

"Oh God." Linda was crying. I could hear it through the phone.

"All these years." She finally spoke. "All these years I thought if we'd just found eight thousand dollars. If I'd just tried harder. If I'd been a better mother—"

"It wouldn't have mattered. Even if we'd paid every penny. Even if I'd answered every call. She still would have killed him. Because he saw her at a murder scene. Because he was a witness."

"Margaret murdered my son." Linda's voice grew harder, angrier. "She murdered my baby because he was in the wrong place."

"Yes."

"What happens now?"

"We're meeting with federal prosecutors in two hours. They'll indict her. Arrest her. This is first-degree murder. She's going to prison for life."

Long silence. Just the sound of Linda crying, processing, grieving all over again.

"I'm sorry. I'm so sorry."

"Don't be sorry. You found the truth. After seven years, you found it." Her voice softened. "Leo would be proud of you. So proud."

In the background, I heard Grace. "Gamma, why are you crying?"

Linda's voice was distant: "I'm okay, baby. Just sad about something. Come here. Let Gamma hold you."

Grace: "Is Mama coming home?"

Linda: "Soon, baby. Mama's doing something very important. Something for Uncle Leo."

Grace: "What?"

Linda: "Making sure the bad people get punished. Making sure Uncle Leo's story is told."

The words broke me. That Grace understood. That Linda was explaining it in a way that made sense. That made this absence mean something.

"I love you," I said. "Both of you."

"We love you too." Linda's voice cracked. "Now go. Go make her pay." We hung up.

I sat there, phone in my hand, crying. Seven years. Seven years of guilt. Of thinking I could have saved him. Of believing the lie about drug debt. And now I knew the truth.

Leo died because he was kind. Because he was harmless. Because even though he was homeless and broken, he still mattered enough to Margaret that she couldn't risk him talking.

Griffin came back out. "Car's ready. We need to go."

The federal building was downtown. Stone and glass, too many flags, security, metal detectors, badges. Elevator to the seventh floor.

A woman met us. Mid-forties, sharp eyes. "Agent Griffin." She shook his hand, then mine. "Ms. Parker. I'm Assistant U.S. Attorney Vanessa Nightingale. I'm very sorry about your brother."

"Thank you."

"Let's get started."

Conference room. Big table. Screens. Three other prosecutors waiting. Griffin set up his laptop and connected it to the screen.

For three hours, Griffin showed them everything: the video, the audio, the texts, the payment. The prosecutors took notes and asked questions.

When Griffin finished, nobody spoke. Vanessa leaned forward. "This is murder. First-degree murder. Conspiracy. Witness tampering."

"Will you prosecute?" I asked.

"We'll destroy her." Vanessa's voice was hard. "This is the clearest case I've seen in years. We have everything."

"When?"

"Grand jury Monday afternoon. We present, they indict, arrest warrant by the end of the day." She looked at Steve. "Ready to testify?"

"Yes."

"Her lawyers will come after you."

"The evidence speaks for itself."

Vanessa looked at me. "Your brother's death is about to become national news. Ready?"

Was I ready? To watch Leo's face everywhere? To hear strangers talk about his addiction? "Yes."

"Good. Because Margaret will fight. She'll claim innocence. She'll attack your brother, make him look unreliable, paint herself as the victim."

"She killed him."

"I know. And we're going to prove it." Vanessa stood. "Monday afternoon. Grand jury. Tuesday morning. Arrest."

We left at 6 PM. The sun was setting, the sky going orange. "Go home. By now, Linda and Grace should be back home safe from the cabin with the FBI agents," Griffin said. "Be with Grace. Monday's grand jury. You don't need to be there."

"And Tuesday?"

"You'll want to see the arrest. But that's Tuesday. You have three days first."

Torres drove me to the airport. He got me a ticket for the 8 PM flight. "She's going down," he said. "For Leo. For Henderson. For everyone."

The plane landed in Cleveland at 10:17 PM. Linda picked me up. Grace was asleep in the car seat. "She cried herself to sleep," Linda said. "She kept asking for you."

"I'm sorry."

"Don't be sorry. You're doing the right thing."

We drove in silence. Linda pulled into the driveway. "Tell me everything. I need to know exactly what happened."

So I did. In the driveway. Grace was sleeping in the back. I recounted the details about the video, about Leo waking up, about the bottle rolling, and about Margaret checking the body. I told her about the audio, Margaret ordering the hit, and the texts. Three days of hunting.

Linda cried through all of it. Quiet tears. The kind that don't stop. When I finished, she said, "He was just sleeping."

"Yes."

"Just trying to survive."

"Yes."

"And she murdered him for it."

"Yes."

We sat there, both crying. Then Linda wiped her face. "Okay. Here's what happens. You go back Tuesday. You watch them arrest her. You do whatever the prosecutors need. And I'll stay here with Grace. Take care of her. Keep her safe."

"She needs her mother."

"She does. But right now, she needs her mother to ensure the woman who killed her uncle goes to prison." Linda looked at me. "This is bigger than us. Bigger than Grace. This is about Leo."

"Mom—"

"I mean it. Stay in Chicago as long as it takes. I've got Grace. You've got Leo."

We got Grace inside and put her to bed. When I came down, Linda was watching the news. Margaret's photo filled the screen.

BREAKING: FEDERAL GRAND JURY TO HEAR MURDER CHARGES

The anchor said, "Sources say a federal grand jury will convene Monday to hear evidence that Margaret Carrington ordered the murder of a homeless man who witnessed a gang execution."

They showed Club Vertical. Then Leo's photo. "The victim has been identified as Leo Parker, 19. Sources say prosecutors have video evidence and audio recordings of Carrington ordering his death."

Linda's hand found mine. The news kept going. Margaret's company. Her empire. Then a commercial. "Everyone will know," Linda said. "About Leo."

"Yes."

"Good. He deserves that. People should know he wasn't just another addict. He was murdered because he saw evil."

Grace called from upstairs. "Mama?"

I went up. She was sitting up, eyes open.

"Hi, baby."

"You came home."

"I promised."

"Are you staying?"

"For the weekend. Then I have to go back. Just for a few days. Then I'm home for good."

Her face fell.

"I know. I'm sorry. But Mama's doing something really important. For Uncle Leo. Remember Uncle Leo?"

"In heaven."

"Yes. In heaven. And Mama's making sure the bad people who hurt him get in trouble."

"Big trouble?"

"Really big trouble."

She looked at me with those eyes. Too old. "Okay," she said. But she didn't believe me. I held her until she fell asleep, then went downstairs.

Linda was still watching the news. Margaret's press conference was on now. Margaret stood outside her building. Perfect. Calm. "These allegations are false. They come from disgruntled employees fabricating evidence."

Pause. "I've built this company over thirty years. And now I'm being targeted with lies. But I'm innocent. And I will prove it."

Reporters shouted questions. Margaret smiled. "The truth will come out."

Linda muted it. "She's lying."

"But she's good at it."

My phone buzzed. Griffin. *Vanessa says Margaret's lawyers filed motions to block the grand jury, claiming evidence was illegally obtained. They're fighting it, but it could delay the process.*

I showed Linda.

"She's trying to stop it."

"Will it work?"

"I don't know."

I looked at Grace's door. "Monday has to work," I said.

Linda nodded. "Get some sleep. Tomorrow, spend the day with Grace. Really be with her before you have to leave again."

"I will."

But I couldn't sleep. I just lay there, staring up, thinking about Leo. Thinking about Grace crying. But I didn't know how to stop it. Because Margaret killed Leo. And someone had to make her pay. Even if it cost everything else.

Chapter Six

6 AM

GRACE WOULDN'T LET GO of my leg. 4:30 AM. Still dark outside. She'd woken up when I was packing and found me in the hallway with my suitcase.

"No. Mama, no." Not screaming. Worse. Quiet. Like she'd already lost and knew it. She wrapped herself around my leg. Three years old. Thirty pounds. But holding on with everything she had.

"Baby, I have to go. Just for two days."

"You said that before." Her voice was so small. "You always say that."

My chest cracked open. Linda came out of her room and saw us in the hallway. Grace clinging to me. Me frozen. I couldn't move. Couldn't make myself peel her off.

"Olivia." Linda's voice was gentle. "Let me take her."

"I can't."

"You have to. The plane leaves in two hours. You'll miss it."

Linda knelt down next to Grace and stroked her hair. "Sweetheart, let Mama go. She has to finish something very important."

"No! She's always leaving!" Grace's voice broke. She started crying. Real sobs. "I want Mama to STAY!"

Every word was a knife. Linda looked at me. Her eyes were wet. "This is for Leo, isn't it? The grand jury?"

I nodded, unable to speak.

"Then you have to go." Linda's voice was firm now. "Leo deserves this. He deserves someone to be there when they finally arrest her."

"But Grace—"

"Grace will be okay. I've got her. We'll go to the playground, get ice cream, watch movies. She'll be okay." Linda touched my face. "But you need to finish this. For your brother. And then you come home and you never leave again."

Linda smiled, sad but real. "Now go. Before you change your mind." She picked up Grace. It took effort. Grace was fighting and screaming now. Linda held her tight.

"I love you, baby," I said, my voice breaking. "Mama loves you so much."

"Then STAY!" Grace reached for me, her little arms stretch-ing. "Mama, please!"

I grabbed my suitcase, walked out the door, and got in my car. Grace's screams followed me down the driveway, down the street, all the way to the highway. Even when I couldn't hear them anymore, they were in my head. I almost turned around.

When they called my boarding group, I stood there, unable to make my legs move. The woman next to me touched my arm. "You okay?"

"My daughter's three. I left her crying this morning."

"Business trip?"

"Something like that."

"It's hard. But they forgive us. Kids always forgive."

I wanted to believe her. Wanted to think Grace would for-give this. But I'd been leaving for months. Over and over. Choosing Chicago over her. Choosing Leo's ghost over her living, breathing need. At what point do kids stop forgiving?

I got on the plane and found my seat. A middle seat. Be-tween a businessman on his laptop and a college kid with headphones.

The businessman looked at me. "You alright?"

That's when I realized I was crying. "Sorry. I'm fine."

"You don't look fine."

The plane took off. Ohio got smaller. I watched Chicago get closer.

Vanessa Nightingale was waiting at the gate when I disembarked.

"Jesus. You look worse than yesterday."

"Grace wouldn't let go of me this morning. I had to leave her screaming."

Vanessa's expression changed. It softened. "How old is she?"

"Three. Almost four."

"I have a six-year-old. Maya. Every time I work late, she asks if I still love her." Vanessa started walking quickly. I had to keep up. "So I get it. The guilt. It's like acid in your stomach."

"Does it get better?"

"No. You just get better at living with it." She led me through security, flashed her badge, and got us through the express line. "But here's what I tell myself: I'm putting monsters in prison so Maya grows up in a world with fewer monsters."

"Does that actually help?"

"Sometimes. When I let myself believe it."

We reached the prosecutor's office. Same beige walls. Same bad coffee. But the energy was different. Electric. People were moving with purpose.

"The grand jury's already seated," Vanessa said. "We're going in thirty minutes."

"What do you need from me?"

"Nothing. Just be here in case they have questions." She paused. "And because when we get the indictment, you should be the first to know. After seven years, you deserve that."

"What if they don't indict?"

"They will. We have video of Margaret ordering a hit, audio recordings, bank transfers, and Steve Adler's testimony. It's airtight."

"Tyler raped me. DNA evidence. Three more victims. And he walked."

Vanessa stopped and looked at me. "That was different. I don't know all the details of that case, but that was local prosecutors scared of Margaret's power. This is federal. We're not scared of her."

"Everyone's scared of her."

"I'm not." Vanessa's voice was firm. Cold. "I watched my dad die of an overdose when I was twelve. I know people like

Margaret Carrington and the gang who killed your brother. So no, I'm not scared. I'm angry."

She walked into a conference room, returned with files, and handed me one. "Read this while you wait. It's everything we're presenting today. All the evidence. Every piece. You should know exactly what we have."

I opened the file. The first page was Leo's photo. The one from his obituary. Smiling. Nineteen. Before he knew what was coming. My hands started shaking.

"You okay?" Vanessa asked.

"No. But I'll read it anyway."

I read the file in that conference room for three hours. Every page made it harder to breathe.

Page 27: Surveillance footage from Club Vertical. April 15th, 2014. 11:43 PM. Leo climbing in through a basement window. Finding a corner. Curling up with his backpack as a pillow. He looked so small. So young. Just trying to find somewhere warm to sleep.

Page 33: The murder. 2:17 AM. Two men dragging a body behind the building. Leo waking up. Seeing them. Making a noise.

The video had no sound, but I could see Leo's face. The terror. He knew. In that moment, he realized he had just witnessed something that would get him killed.

Page 41: Margaret arrives. Black car. Designer coat. She walked to the body, checked it, made a phone call, and looked around.

Page 58: The hunt. Three days of texts to her security team. *Find the witness. Find the homeless boy. He can't be allowed to testify.*

We thought Leo was the problem. We didn't know he was the victim.

Page 89: April 18th, 2014. Midnight. Behind the warehouse on Fifth Street. Where they found him. The gunshot that killed Leo. I closed the file, ran to the bathroom, and threw up everything in my stomach, kept heaving even after there was nothing left.

At 1:47 PM, Vanessa burst through the door. "We got it."

My heart stopped. "Unanimous. All twenty-three votes." She was smiling. Fierce. Victorious. "First-degree murder. Conspiracy. RICO. Obstruction. The grand jury indicted her on everything."

"So she's going to prison?"

"If we win at trial, yes. Life without parole." Vanessa sat down and pulled out a folder. "The indictment means we have enough evidence to charge her. Now we arrest her, arraign her, and build our case for trial."

My stomach dropped. "Trial? I thought the indictment meant—"

"The indictment means a jury of citizens believes there's probable cause, that we have enough evidence to proceed. But we still have to prove her guilt beyond a reasonable doubt in front of twelve jurors."

"How long does that take?"

"Months. Maybe a year. Margaret's lawyers will file every motion possible, try to suppress evidence, delay proceedings, and get charges dismissed." Vanessa leaned forward. "But we have video of her ordering a hit, audio recordings, bank transfers, and Steve Adler's testimony. It's the strongest case I've ever built."

"What if she gets bail?"

"She won't. Not for first-degree murder. Not with her resources. She's a massive flight risk." Vanessa's face was hard. "Tomorrow we arrest her. She'll be arraigned in the afternoon. The judge will deny bail, and she'll sit in federal detention until trial."

I should've felt relief, but all I felt was exhaustion. "So it's not over."

"The investigation is over. The arrest is tomorrow. But the trial?" Vanessa shook her head. "That's just beginning. And Margaret will fight like hell. She'll hire the best lawyers money can buy. They'll attack every piece of evidence and every witness."

My hands clenched. "They can't do that."

"They can and they will. That's their job." Vanessa's voice softened. "But our job is to make sure the jury sees the truth: that Leo was a nineteen-year-old kid who witnessed a murder, and Margaret Carrington had him executed to protect herself."

"Will you win?"

"Yes. But it won't be easy." She stood. "Tomorrow at 6 AM, we arrest her. Do you want to be there?"

"I can't be at the actual arrest, can I?"

"No. It's an active operation. Dangerous. But we'll have cameras. Live feeds." She paused. "I can let you watch from the command center if you want."

My throat closed up. "Thank you."

"Don't thank me yet. We still have months of fighting ahead." She headed for the door. "Get some rest. Tomorrow's going to be a long day."

"Vanessa?"

She turned.

"Thank you very much. I really mean it."

"You're welcome." She left. I sat there staring at the file. At Leo's face. At the evidence that should be enough but might not be. Because I'd learned the hard way. Evidence didn't always matter. Tyler had DNA evidence. A rape kit. Victims. And he walked. What if Margaret walked too?

I walked around Chicago for hours. Past Carrington Media headquarters, where Margaret built her empire on blood. I kept walking and ended up at the Peninsula Hotel. The same brand of hotel where I'd had my breakdown six years ago in Chicago. Where my life fell apart. I booked a room on the same floor. Hard to tell.

I couldn't sleep. I lay there staring at the ceiling, thinking about Leo's face in that video. At 2 AM, I gave up on sleep. I showered, got dressed, and sat by the window watching the city wake up. At 4:30, my phone rang. Griffin.

"You coming?"

"Yeah."

"Good. Because Vanessa told me what you said about wanting to be there for the arrest." His voice was gentle. "That takes guts. Watching your brother's killer get handcuffed. Not everyone could handle that."

"I have to. He deserves someone there."

"He does. And you're a good sister for being that someone."

"I wasn't a good sister. That's the problem."

"You are now. That counts for something."

"Does it?"

"We'll find out in two hours."

The FBI command center looked like a war room. Screens everywhere. Maps. Live feeds. Agents in tactical gear checking weapons. Griffin led me to a desk in the back corner. Three monitors. Headphones.

He handed me the headphones. "The FBI agents will have body cameras. You'll hear everything, see everything. But Olivia? If it gets too intense, you can leave. No one will judge you."

"I'm not leaving."

"Okay. But maybe don't watch alone." He pulled up a chair and sat next to me. "I'll stay, just in case."

Vanessa came over and handed me coffee. "You ready for this?"

"No. But I'm doing it anyway."

5:47 AM. The teams moved into position. I watched on the screens. Black SUVs parked on both streets. Agents flooded out. Weapons drawn. Moving like a machine. My hands shook so badly I had to put the coffee down.

5:52. The radio crackled. "All units in position."

5:55. "Margaret's security changed shifts. We're clear."

5:58. "Tyler's doorman on a smoke break. Window's open."

Griffin looked at me. "Last chance to change your mind."

"I'm staying."

6:00 AM exactly. The radio: "Execute. Execute. Execute." Both teams moved simultaneously. Doors kicked open. Agents flooded in, shouting, "FBI! Don't move!"

Tyler raised his hands slowly, deliberately. "What is this about?"

"Tyler Carrington, you're under arrest for conspiracy to obstruct justice and witness tampering."

His face went blank. Professional. Like he'd prepared for this moment. "I need to call my lawyer."

"You can call from the station. Hands behind your back."

They cuffed him. He didn't resist. Didn't fight. Just stood there in his expensive pajamas. Silk. Probably cost more than most people's rent.

"This is my mother's doing," he said, his voice calm, almost bored. "Whatever she told you. Whatever evidence you think you have. She manipulated me. Used me."

"Save it for your lawyer."

This was the man who raped me. Who tied me down while Bach played. Who smiled at me in that courthouse hallway. Who made Grace without my consent. And he looked perfectly calm. Like getting arrested was just another inconvenience in his carefully planned life.

"You ready?" the agent asked.

"As ready as one can be for false imprisonment." Tyler's voice was cold, certain. "My lawyers will have me out by noon."

"We'll see about that."

They led him to the door. His eyes were empty. Not scared. Not angry. Just calculating. Like he was already planning his next move. Then he smiled. Small. Cold. Just like his mother.

6:17 AM. Both in custody. Both being led to vehicles. The center screen showed both streets. News vans everywhere. Cameras. Reporters. Someone had leaked the timing.

Margaret walked out first. Head high. Handcuffs behind her back. She stopped at the top of the steps, looked directly at the cameras, and smiled. Cold. Perfect. Unbroken. Like this was just another photo op for the media empire she built.

Then Tyler. He didn't hide his face. Didn't hunch over. Walked out like he owned the building. Suit perfect. Hair perfect. Handcuffs the only thing that looked wrong. He stopped at the top of the steps, looked at the cameras, and spoke. I couldn't hear what he said, but I read his lips: "This is a mistake. I'll be home tonight."

Then they led him to the car. He got in smoothly. No struggle. No shame. Grace's biological father being led away in handcuffs. But he didn't look defeated. He looked patient. Like he was waiting for something.

I watched both screens. Margaret composed. Tyler composed. Mother and son. Both refusing to break. Both believing they'd win. And I realized something that made my chest hurt. Grace was going to see this someday. She'd be older, old enough to understand. And she'd ask me why her father was arrested.

What would I tell her? That her father was like her grandmother? Cold. Calculating. Dangerous even in handcuffs. That power and money didn't make people humble; it made them believe they were untouchable.

Griffin took off his headphones. "It's over. They're in custody. Both of them."

"Yeah."

"You okay?"

"No. But I don't think I'm supposed to be."

My phone buzzed. Linda. *Grace just woke up. The first thing she said was, "Is Mama catching bad people done yet?" What do I tell her?*

I looked at the screens. Margaret in one car. Tyler in another. Both driving away. To jail. To arraignment. To justice. Leo's justice. But not Grace's peace.

I typed back: *Tell her Mama's coming home. Tell her I'm done.*

Vanessa came over. "Arraignment is at 2 PM. You should be there. The judge will set bail. Probably denied for both. But you should see it."

"I can't. I have to go home."

"Olivia, this is the culmination of everything. You built this case. You deserve to see it through."

"I know. But my daughter deserves her mother more."

I stood up, grabbed my bag, and looked at Griffin. "Thank you. For letting me watch. For being here."

"You're leaving? Now?"

"Now. Before I change my mind again."

I was at the door when Vanessa called out. "Olivia! The next time you doubt whether this mattered, remember something. Leo died thinking no one cared. That he was nothing. Just another dead junkie. But today, the FBI arrested a billionaire for his murder. Today, the federal government said his life mattered. That's because of you."

My eyes burned. "Will that matter to Grace?"

"I don't know. But maybe someday it will matter to her."

I walked out, through Federal Plaza, through security, and out into the morning light. Chicago was waking up. People everywhere. Living their normal lives. Not knowing that somewhere in this city, Margaret Carrington was sitting in a federal holding cell. That Tyler was breaking down in another. That justice had been served.

I took a cab to the airport, got there by 9 AM, bought a ticket for the first flight home. 11:15 departure. I sat at the gate. CNN was on the airport TV. I couldn't look away.

BREAKING NEWS: BILLIONAIRE CEO ARRESTED FOR MURDER

Margaret's face filled the screen. Her perp walk. Head high. Smiling at the cameras. Like she was walking a red carpet instead of into a police car. Then Tyler. Face hidden. Body hunched. Broken. Then Leo's face. His obituary photo. Nineteen years old. Smiling. Before the drugs. Before Margaret. Before everything.

"Leo Parker was murdered in 2014 behind a warehouse in Millfield, Ohio," the anchor said. "For seven years, police believed it was gang-related. But federal prosecutors now say he witnessed a murder and was killed to silence him. Margaret Carrington, CEO of Carrington Media, allegedly ordered the hit. She faces life in prison if convicted."

My phone rang. Unknown number. Millfield area code.

"Hello?"

"Olivia Parker?"

"Yeah."

"This is Detective Doyle. I'm the one who investigated your brother's case back in 2014."

My chest tightened. I remembered him. The detective who told me about the eight thousand dollars. Who said Leo had died believing I'd save him.

"I wanted to call and tell you..." His voice cracked. "I'm sorry. We got it wrong. I got it wrong. I believed it was just drug debt. Gang violence. I didn't look deeper. Didn't push harder."

"It's okay."

"It's not okay. Your brother deserved better. He deserved a real investigation. And if I'd done my job right seven years ago, maybe Margaret would've been arrested then. Maybe other people wouldn't have died."

"You couldn't have known."

"That's what I tell myself. But it doesn't help." He was quiet. Then: "I'm glad they finally got her. I'm glad Leo is getting justice. He was a good kid. He had a good heart."

"Thank you for saying that."

"It's true. And Olivia? I read the file and now know the details. Now, I hope you don't blame yourself anymore. You couldn't have known either."

After he hung up, I sat there in the airport crying. People walked past, staring. A woman stopped. "You okay?"

"My brother. On the news. That was my brother."

Her face changed. Softened. "I'm so sorry."

"He's been dead seven years. Today they arrested the person who killed him."

"Then why are you crying?"

"I don't know... I don't know."

The woman sat down next to me without asking for permission. "My dad was murdered when I was seven," she said quietly. "It took fifteen years to catch the guy. By then, I was married. Had kids of my own. A whole life he never saw."

She paused and looked at me. "When they finally arrested him, I felt nothing. Just... empty. Like it came too late to matter."

"So it doesn't get better? Justice doesn't actually help?"

"I didn't say that." She pulled out a tissue and handed it to me. "My dad died thinking nobody cared. That he didn't matter enough for anyone to keep looking. But someone did keep looking. For fifteen years. And when they caught the guy, I realized that my dad was wrong. He mattered. Someone fought for him."

"Even though he wasn't there to see it?"

"Especially because he wasn't there to see it." She stood and smiled sadly. "Your brother believed someone would save him. And you did. Just not in time. But you still did it." She walked away.

I sat there for another minute, watching people rush past. Everyone going somewhere. Everyone with their own emergencies, grief, and normal lives.

My boarding group was called. I grabbed my bag and found my seat. The plane took off. Chicago got smaller below. I was going home. To Grace. To Linda. To whatever came next. Margaret was arrested. Tyler was arrested. Leo was close to getting justice. Only trials left. But I couldn't shake the feeling that I'd lost something in the process. Something I might not get back.

The woman next to me was reading her phone. I caught a glimpse of the screen. A headline: **CARRINGTON ARREST: Media Billionaire Charged in Decade-Old Murder.**

Leo's face was there, next to Margaret's and Tyler's. His nineteen-year-old smile frozen forever. Below it, another headline: **Justice After 7 Years: Homeless Teen's Sister Never Stopped Fighting.**

I closed my eyes. The rest would have to wait until I got home.

Chapter Seven

The Trials

I WAS HOME WITH Grace, making breakfast: toast with butter cut into triangles the way she liked. The kitchen smelled like coffee and burned edges. Normal things. Safe things.

My phone lit up. Vanessa Nightingale. "We have the trial dates."

The spatula clattered on the floor. Grace looked up from her coloring book, orange crayon frozen mid-stroke.

"That's great. When's the trial?"

"Margaret's starts in two weeks. Federal court moves fast when they want someone. Tyler's is separate. Six weeks out."

Two weeks. Seven years of waiting, and now two weeks. Grace was staring at me. "Mama?"

I couldn't answer her. I couldn't breathe.

"You'll need to testify," Vanessa said. "About Leo. About what you know. About Margaret's threats. It won't be easy."

"Okay."

"Her lawyers will come after you. Everything. Your past. Your addiction. Your connection to Tyler. They'll make it ugly."

I looked at Grace. Three years old. Almost four. Yellow crayon now. Drawing a sun with too many rays. She had no idea the people who killed Uncle Leo were finally going to answer for it.

"I don't care," I said. "Whatever you need. I'll do it."

After I hung up, Grace climbed into my lap. "Why are you shaking?"

"Just cold, baby."

"It's not cold."

"I know."

She put her small hand on my cheek. Warm. Real. "The bad people?"

"Yeah. The bad people are going to court."

"They will cry?"

"I hope so."

She thought about this. Then went back to her coloring, as if the world hadn't just shifted on its axis. Linda found me still sitting there twenty minutes later. Grace had moved on to playing with blocks. I was frozen, staring at nothing.

"Olivia?"

"Two weeks. Margaret's trial in two weeks."

She sat down across from me. "We have to go together."

"Yes, we have to."

"For Leo."

We sat there in silence. Grace was building a tower, knocking it down, and rebuilding it. Not knowing her mama was about to leave again. Hopefully, for the last time.

The federal courthouse looked like something built to intimidate: stone columns, high windows, American flags snapping in the wind. Linda met me at the entrance. Her flight had landed twenty minutes before mine.

"Ready?" she asked.

"No."

"Me either."

We went through security: metal detectors, ID checks, armed guards everywhere. Like we were entering a fortress.

The courtroom was on the third floor, Room 317. The hallway outside was packed with people: reporters, cameras, spectators trying to get in. A reporter recognized me. "Ms. Parker! Will you be testifying?"

I kept walking.

"Ms. Parker! Do you think Margaret Carrington will be convicted?"

Linda grabbed my arm and pulled me through the crowd.

Inside, the courtroom was massive, with wood paneling everywhere. It was dark and heavy, the ceiling rising to a height of twenty feet. Rows of benches resembled church pews. A judge's bench at the front was elevated, looking down on everyone. The jury box sat empty on the right: twelve chairs for twelve strangers who'd never met Leo, who would decide if his death mattered.

Linda and I found seats in the gallery. Fifth row back. Close enough to see everything but far enough to feel invisible. People filled in around us, packing the benches. It was standing room only. Everyone wanted to see Margaret Carrington go down.

At 9:27 AM, a side door opened, and Margaret walked in. She wore gray. Not designer clothes. Simple. Conservative. A blouse and slacks that could have come from Macy's. Her hair was pulled back in a low bun, with no jewelry except small pearl earrings. She was trying to look humble, but it didn't work. You could still see it: that arrogance, that certainty. The way she held herself suggested she owned the room, even in handcuffs.

Four lawyers followed her, all men in expensive suits. Richard Sterling led the group, with silver hair and tanned skin, his voice smooth like honey. They sat at the defense table, and the bailiff removed Margaret's handcuffs. She rubbed her wrists slowly and deliberately, ensuring the jury would see the red marks when they came in. Then she turned, her eyes sweeping the gallery until they found me.

She stared. Not angry. Not hateful. Just cold. Calculating. Like I was a business problem she was figuring out how to solve. Five seconds. Ten. Fifteen. People around us shifted, uncomfortable, sensing something passing between us that they couldn't understand. Margaret didn't blink or look away. I held her gaze, matching that predator stare.

Linda grabbed my hand. "Don't."

"Don't what?"

"Whatever you're thinking. Don't."

Margaret's mouth curved. Not quite a smile, just an acknowledgment, as if she'd confirmed something about me that was useful. Then Sterling leaned over and whispered in her ear. She nodded and turned back around, composed and perfect.

My hands were shaking, so I sat on them. "She's trying to rattle you," Linda whispered.

"It's working."

At 9:30, the bailiff stood. "All rise." Everyone stood. The rustling of fabric, feet shuffling, someone coughing.

Judge Kline entered, an older Black man with a gray beard and tired eyes, as if he had seen too many cases like this and knew how they usually ended.

"Be seated." Everyone sat, the benches creaking. I could smell wood polish and something else. Fear, maybe. Sweat. The recycled air of too many people in one space.

"We're here for the case of United States versus Margaret Carrington," the judge said, his voice deep and measured. "Is the prosecution ready?"

Vanessa Nightingale stood. "Yes, Your Honor," she said, in a sharp black suit, her hair pulled back tight, exuding no nonsense.

"Is the defense ready?" Sterling stood, smiling. "Yes, Your Honor."

"Then let's bring in the jury."

The side door opened. Twelve people filed in: seven women and five men of mixed ages and races. They looked nervous and excited, as if they knew they were part of something important. They sat in the jury box, arranged themselves, and found their seats. Notebooks appeared. Pens. Everyone was ready to judge.

The judge gave instructions about reasonable doubt, the presumption of innocence, and how evidence works. Legal language that meant nothing and everything.

I stopped listening and just watched Margaret. She sat perfectly still, hands folded on the table, posture straight, looking ahead at the judge like a model student. But I noticed her jaw tighten when the judge said "criminal enterprise," and her fingers tensed when he said "murder." Small things. Things no one else would notice. But I'd been watching her for years. I knew her tells. She was scared; she just hid it better than anyone I'd ever seen.

"Ms. Nightingale," the judge said. "Opening statement."

Vanessa stood, buttoned her jacket, and walked to the jury box. She didn't smile or try to be friendly. She looked at them like they were soldiers she was about to send into battle.

"Margaret Carrington built an empire," she said, her voice strong and clear. "But she built it on blood."

She walked the length of the jury box, her heels clicking on the hardwood with each deliberate step. "On the deaths of innocent people. On covering up her son's crimes. On money laundering that funded gang violence across six cities. On ordering hits on anyone who threatened to expose her."

She stopped, turned, and pointed at Margaret. "The evidence will show that Margaret Carrington isn't a businesswoman. She's a criminal, a murderer, and she belongs in prison."

Margaret didn't move or react; she just sat there with that blank face. But her hand found Sterling's arm under the table. I saw it, the way her knuckles went white, the way she gripped him like he was the only thing keeping her upright.

Vanessa continued, walking them through it: the clubs, the gang connections, the money laundering, Steve Adler's testimony, the bank transfers, Leo's death.

Eleven minutes. That's all it took to lay out seven years of Margaret's crimes. When Vanessa sat down, the courtroom was silent.

Then Sterling stood. He smiled at the jury, warm and friendly, as if they were old friends meeting for coffee.

"Margaret Carrington is sixty-two years old," he said, his voice smooth and easy. "She's built one of the most successful media companies in the world: eight thousand employees and millions in charitable donations. A mother, a grandmother, a woman who started with nothing and built everything."

He walked toward the jury, casual and relaxed. "And the prosecution wants you to believe she's a murderer. Based on what?"

He turned and looked right at me in the gallery. "Based on the testimony of Steve Adler, a man who admitted to cooking her books for twelve years, a confessed criminal, a liar who got caught and tried to blame his boss to save himself."

My face burned. "Based on the word of Olivia Parker—" He said my name like it was something dirty. "—a woman with a prostitution record and a personal vendetta against this family."

Margaret was watching me. I could feel it, not directly, just peripherally, as if she wanted to see if Sterling's words landed. They did. I felt them like stones.

"This case is about desperation," Sterling said, walking back to the jury box. "About people trying to destroy an innocent woman because they need someone to blame for their own failures. For their own choices."

He paused at each word, letting them sink in. "Steve Adler stole from his employer for years. He got caught. Now he's trying to trade his boss for a lighter sentence."

Another pause. "Olivia Parker ignored her brother's calls for weeks. She let him die when she had the money to save him. Now she needs someone to blame for that guilt."

My hands curled into fists. Linda grabbed one and held it tight.

Sterling walked back to the defense table and put his hand on Margaret's shoulder. Gentle. Protective. "Margaret Carrington is innocent. And by the end of this trial, you'll see that clearly."

He sat down. The judge looked at the clock. "We'll take a fifteen-minute recess." Everyone stood. The courtroom erupted in noise: people talking, moving, heading for the doors.

Linda pulled me up. "Bathroom. Now." We pushed through the crowd, down the hallway, into the women's bathroom. It was empty. Linda checked the stalls, then turned to me.

"You okay?"

"No."

"Sterling's going to do that every time you're mentioned. You ready for that?"

"I don't know."

"You need to be."

I went to the sink and ran cold water over my wrists. The shock of it helped. A little. I looked at myself in the mirror. Pale. Dark circles like bruises. Hair pulled back so tight my scalp ached. I looked like someone hanging on by threads.

The door opened. Margaret walked in. Time stopped.

She saw me. Her expression didn't change. Not surprise. Not anger. Nothing. Like she'd been expecting this. Like she'd planned it. We stared at each other across six feet of white tile. The fluorescent lights hummed. Water dripped from my wrists into the sink. Linda stepped forward, positioning herself between us. "You need to leave. Now."

Margaret's smile was small. Cold. "It's a public bathroom, Linda. I'm allowed to wash my hands." She walked to the sink, two sinks down from me. Close enough to make my skin crawl but far enough to seem reasonable. She turned on the water and washed her hands slowly, deliberately, like she had all the time in the world. Neither of us moved.

Margaret looked at me in the mirror. Our eyes met in the reflection. "You know you're going to lose."

My throat closed. My heart hammered against my ribs.

"Margaret—" Linda started.

"Not you." Margaret's eyes stayed locked on mine in the glass. "Her. She knows. Deep down, where she can't lie to herself anymore, she knows I'm going to walk out of here. Free."

"They indicted you on twelve counts," I said, my voice shaking, hating that she could hear it tremble. "The jury's going to hear everything. Every crime. Every murder. Everything."

"The jury's going to hear a sex worker with a grudge and a criminal trying to save himself from prison." She turned off the water and dried her hands on a paper towel. Each movement was precise. Controlled. "That's all they'll remember. That's all that matters."

She threw the paper towel in the trash and turned to face me directly. Not in the mirror anymore. Real. "You should have taken my advice years ago. Should've disappeared with that settlement money. Started over somewhere I'd never find you." Her voice grew quieter. Harder. "Instead, you bought my stock. Started this war. Thought you could destroy me. And now?"

She stepped closer, close enough that I could smell her perfume. Something expensive. Floral. The same perfume that was probably on her clothes when she watched her people put a gun to Leo's head.

My stomach turned.

"Now you're going to sit in that courtroom every single day for weeks. Months, maybe. Watching me walk free. Watching your brother's killer smile for the cameras. And then you're going to go home to your daughter—" She paused. Let it sink in. "And explain why Mama wasted years chasing revenge instead of being her mother."

My hand moved before I thought, before I could stop myself. I drew back, ready to slap that perfect calm off her face. Margaret didn't flinch. Didn't step back. Just smiled wider.

"Do it," she whispered, her voice soft, almost encouraging. "Hit me. Give me bruises to show the jury. Assault and battery against a defendant. Make me the victim. Make yourself the violent, unstable woman Sterling says you are."

Linda grabbed my arm hard enough to hurt. "Don't. Olivia, don't."

The bathroom door opened. A court officer peeked in, looked between us, and saw the tension. "Trial's resuming in two minutes. You need to be in your seats."

Margaret walked past me, close enough that her shoulder almost brushed mine. She stopped at the door and looked back.

"See you in there, Olivia." Her smile was genuine now, as if she'd won something. "I'll be the one walking out at the end.

You'll be the one explaining to Grace why Mama broke her promises." Then, she was gone.

I stood there shaking, my whole body trembling, hands gripping the sink so hard my knuckles turned white. Linda held me. "She's trying to make you lose control. That's all this was. Don't let her."

"She's right." The words came out broken. "About all of it. Steve's crimes. The jury will see exactly what Sterling wants them to see."

"No." Linda's voice was fierce. Firm. "She's scared. That's why she came in here. Not to gloat, but to rattle you before you testify. Because she knows Steve's testimony will be solid and yours will destroy her."

"Will it?"

"Yes." Linda grabbed my face and made me look at her. "Because you're telling the truth. And she's terrified of the truth. Terrified enough to risk witness tampering, to corner you in a bathroom, to threaten you. That's not confidence. That's fear."

"What if the jury doesn't believe me? What if they think—"

"Then we fight harder. But you don't let her win before you even testify. You don't give her that." Linda's eyes were wet. "Leo deserves better. Grace deserves better. You deserve better."

We went back to the courtroom and found our seats. My hands were still shaking. Margaret was already at the defense table. Composed. Perfect. Hair still in place. Makeup still flawless. Like nothing happened. Like she hadn't just threatened me. Like she hadn't just smiled while talking about my daughter.

She glanced at me once. Just once. And smiled that same cold smile. But I saw her hand. Under the table where the jury couldn't see. Shaking. Just a little. Just enough.

Linda was right. Margaret wasn't confident. She was scared. And scared people make mistakes. Good. Let her shake. Let her be scared. Because I was terrified. But I was still here. Still standing. Still fighting. For Leo. For Grace. For everyone Margaret thought didn't matter. Let her shake.

Steve testified first. He came in wearing a navy suit that hung loose on his frame. He'd lost weight. Maybe thirty pounds. The surgery had taken something from him, leaving him smaller and older. The bailiff swore him in. He sat in the witness box and adjusted the microphone. His hands trembled.

Vanessa walked him through it slowly and methodically. "Mr. Adler, how long did you work for Carrington Media?"

"Twelve years."

"In what capacity?"

"Chief Financial Officer."

"And in that role, what were your responsibilities?"

"I managed all financial operations: accounting, financial reporting, and banking relationships."

"Did those responsibilities include processing transactions through the company's nightclub division?"

"Yes."

"Can you describe those transactions?"

Steve took a breath. "Starting in 2013, I processed large cash deposits from the clubs: Club Vertical in Millfield, Ohio; Club Meridian in Detroit; Club Seven in Milwaukee; and five others."

"How large were these deposits?"

"Between fifty thousand and two hundred thousand per month, per club."

"That's a lot of cash for nightclubs."

"Yes."

"Did that seem unusual to you?"

"At first. But Ms. Carrington explained they were high-volume establishments."

"Did you believe that?"

Steve looked at Margaret. She stared back, cold and empty. "No," he said quietly. "I knew what they were. Money laundering operations. I just didn't want to admit it."

"Objection," Sterling said. "Speculation."

"I'll allow it," the judge said. "The witness can testify to his own beliefs."

Vanessa pulled up a document on the screen. "Mr. Adler, do you recognize this?"

"Yes. That's a wire transfer authorization from April 2014."

"Can you read the amount?"

"One hundred thousand dollars."

"And the recipient?"

"Meridian Holdings LLC."

"Do you know what Meridian Holdings is?"

"Yes." Steve's voice got quieter. "It's a shell company used by the Scorpions gang for money laundering."

"And whose signature is on this authorization?"

"Margaret Carrington's."

The courtroom was silent. You could hear the air conditioning and the scratch of a reporter's pen.

I watched Margaret. She sat perfectly still, but her jaw tightened. Her hand gripped the edge of the table. Her breathing changed. Shallow, faster.

Vanessa pulled up more documents: transaction after transaction, all with Margaret's signature, all going to gang-connected shell companies.

"Over eight years," Vanessa said, "how much money did Carrington Media transfer to these organizations?"

"Approximately 10 million dollars."

"And did Ms. Carrington know where this money was going?"

"Yes."

"How do you know?"

"Because I asked her directly in March 2015. I said the transactions looked suspicious. She said—" He paused. "She said, 'Steve, some business relationships are complicated. All you need to do is process the paperwork and keep your mouth shut.'"

Margaret leaned forward. She whispered to Sterling. Her face was still blank, but her hand was shaking. Actually shaking.

Vanessa pulled up a photo. "Do you recognize this location?"

"Yes. That's Club Vertical in Millfield, Ohio."

"And do you know what happened there on April 14, 2014?"

"Yes. A murder. A gang-connected murder in the building."

"And four days later?"

Steve's voice broke. "Another murder. Leo Parker. Shot in the head. Execution style. By the same gang."

"The gang that received money from Margaret Carrington after Leo died?"

"Yes."

"Objection!" Sterling was on his feet. "There's no evidence connecting these transactions to Mr. Parker's death."

"Your Honor," Vanessa said calmly, "the witness is testifying to the timeline. The jury can draw their own conclusions."

"I'll allow it. But Mr. Sterling's objection is noted."

The rest of Steve's testimony lasted two more hours. Vanessa walked him through every transaction, every document, every signature. By the end, the jury looked exhausted, overwhelmed by the sheer volume of evidence.

Then came Sterling's cross-examination. He stood slowly, smiling at Steve like they were old friends. "Mr. Adler, you admitted to committing fraud for twelve years, correct?"

"Yes."

"You lied to investigators."

"Yes."

"You lied to shareholders."

"Yes."

"You lied to federal regulators."

"Yes."

Sterling walked closer. "So why should this jury believe you're telling the truth now?"

The question hung in the air. Everyone was waiting. Steve looked at Margaret, then at the jury. "Because I'm done lying." His voice cracked.

"Because people died. Because I watched Margaret order hits, and I stayed silent. Because I helped her launder money that funded gangs that killed innocent people, including a nineteen-year-old kid who was just trying to stay alive."

He wiped his eyes. "Because I can't stay silent anymore. Because I have to live with what I did. And the only way I can live with it is by telling the truth."

Sterling smiled. "How convenient. Right when you got caught."

"Maybe." Steve met his gaze. "But it's still the truth."

Margaret leaned forward, whispering urgently to Sterling. He nodded and turned back to Steve.

"You're testifying here today because prosecutors offered you a deal, correct?"

"Yes."

"They're recommending a reduced sentence in exchange for your cooperation?"

"Yes."

"So you have a strong motivation to blame Ms. Carrington."

"I have a strong motivation to tell the truth."

"Or to tell a story that gets you out of prison faster."

"I'm going to prison either way. For years. This isn't about me. It's about stopping her."

Steve pointed at Margaret. "It's about making sure she can't hurt anyone else."

Sterling spent three more hours trying to break him, attempting to make him look like a liar, a coward, a criminal trying to save himself. But Steve didn't break. He just kept answering, kept telling the truth. By the end, even Sterling looked tired.

The judge called a recess for the day. "We'll resume tomorrow morning. Nine AM." Everyone stood, and the courtroom emptied slowly.

Linda and I stayed in our seats, watching Margaret leave with her lawyers. She looked exhausted. For the first time, genuinely exhausted.

"She's losing," Linda whispered.

"Maybe."

"You saw the jury. They believed him."

"Some of them."

"That's enough."

We left the courthouse. The sun was setting, Chicago lights coming on, the city transforming from day to night. Cars streamed past, and people were everywhere. The city was alive and moving.

Linda touched my arm. "You okay?"

"I'm fine."

"This will be over soon. Then we can all go home together."

Chapter Eight

The Others

JESSICA TESTIFIED ON DAY two. I hadn't seen her since the settlement meeting years ago. She looked different. Stronger. Hair shorter. Dressed in a simple black suit. No jewelry. She walked to the witness stand like she was walking into battle.

Vanessa stood. "Ms. Ramirez, can you tell the jury how you know Tyler Carrington?"

"We went to Northwestern together. Same year."

"And did you have a relationship?"

"No. We were acquaintances. We ran in overlapping social circles."

"When did that change?"

Jessica's hands gripped the armrests. "March 2016. Tyler invited me to dinner. He said he wanted to discuss a start-up idea. I was interested in entrepreneurship."

"Where did you go?"

"A restaurant in downtown Chicago. Italian. Expensive."

"What happened?"

Jessica took a breath. "We had dinner. Wine. He ordered a bottle. I had maybe two glasses. Then he suggested we go back to his apartment to look at some business plans."

She paused. The courtroom was silent.

"What happened at the apartment?"

"He poured more wine. I remember drinking it. I remember feeling dizzy. Then I don't remember anything."

"When did you wake up?"

"Hours later. It was dark. I was in his bed. My clothes were disheveled. Blood on my thighs. Pain everywhere."

I watched Margaret. She was taking notes. Her pen moved across the paper. Her face was blank, like she was listening to a weather report. But her hand. That same white-knuckled grip on the pen. The way her jaw tightened. The way she shifted in her seat.

"What did you do?" Vanessa asked.

"I got dressed. Tried to leave. Tyler woke up. He said—" Her voice caught. "He said, 'Whoa, you really can't handle your alcohol. You should probably go.'"

"Did he acknowledge what happened?"

"No. He acted like I'd just passed out drunk. Like nothing else happened."

"What did you do next?"

"I went home. Took a shower. Tried to scrub it off. Then I just... sat there. Trying to figure out what to do."

"Did you report it?"

"No."

"Why not?"

"Because I couldn't remember. I had gaps. Hours missing. And Tyler was Tyler Carrington. His mother runs Carrington Media. They had money. Lawyers. Power. I was a graduate student with forty thousand in debt."

"What did you do?"

"I tried to forget. Graduated. Got a job. Moved on with my life. Or tried to."

Vanessa pulled up a document. "Ms. Ramirez, when did you first come forward publicly about what happened to you?"

"2019. I saw an article in the Chicago Tribune about Olivia Parker. About Tyler. About how he'd done this before."

"What made you decide to come forward?"

Jessica's voice got quieter. "I realized I wasn't the only one. That Tyler had a pattern. That if I stayed quiet, there would be more."

"What happened after you came forward?"

"I lost my job the day the article was published. They said it was budget cuts, but I knew why. I sent out over two hundred applications after that and got three interviews, but no offers."

Her hands tightened on the armrests.

"I received an eviction notice. I couldn't make rent. I'd been homeless before, years earlier, and I was terrified of going back to that. The shelters. The fear. The way people look through you like you don't exist."

"Did anyone from the Carrington family contact you after you came forward?"

"Yes, a lawyer. Richard Sterling."

Sterling shifted in his seat, uncomfortable.

"When did Mr. Sterling contact you?"

"A few weeks after I came forward publicly. He called a meeting with me, Olivia, and two other women who'd also accused Tyler. All four of us together."

"What happened at that meeting?"

"Margaret Carrington was there, along with her lawyers. They offered us a settlement. Two million dollars each to sign non-disclosure agreements and stop cooperating with the criminal investigation."

"Did you accept?"

Jessica's eyes went to Margaret, then back to the jury.

"Yes."

"Why?"

Her voice cracked. "Because I had no choice. I'd lost everything."

"What do you mean?"

"I'd lost my job, I was facing eviction, and I had no money or prospects. They told us the criminal case would take years with no guarantee of conviction."

"So you signed the agreement?"

"Yes. I moved to Seattle and tried to start over."

"Did you succeed?"

"No." Jessica's voice broke. "You don't forget being raped. You don't forget being drugged and violated. The money just meant I could be scared in a nicer apartment."

"Why are you testifying today? You signed a non-disclosure agreement."

Jessica looked at Margaret again, really looked at her.

"Because NDAs don't cover testimony in criminal proceedings. Because I watched Margaret use her wealth and power to protect a serial rapist for years."

She turned to the jury. "She paid eight million dollars total to make four rape victims disappear, to let Tyler keep living his life, to ensure he never faced consequences."

The courtroom was silent.

Vanessa nodded. "Thank you, Ms. Ramirez. No further questions."

Sterling stood for cross-examination. "Ms. Ramirez, you testified that you don't remember what happened that night, correct?"

"I remember being drugged."

"But you don't remember the actual assault?"

"No."

"So you have no direct evidence that Mr. Tyler Carrington raped you?"

"I have gaps in my memory and the fact that he drugged me."

"Or you had too much to drink, made a mistake, and now you're trying to—"

"Objection!" Vanessa was on her feet. "Counsel is badgering the witness."

"Sustained. Mr. Sterling, move on."

But the damage was done. The jury had heard it. The suggestion that Jessica was lying, mistaken, or drunk. Sterling kept going. "You came forward publicly through the media before any criminal charges were filed, correct?"

"Yes."

"And you did this knowing it might cost you your job?"

"I did it because it was the right thing to do."

"But then you took two million dollars from my client."

"After I lost my job. After I was facing eviction. After your client used her power to destroy my life for telling the truth."

Sterling's voice sharpened. "You signed a non-disclosure agreement. You agreed not to discuss these allegations."

"I agreed not to discuss them publicly. I didn't agree to lie under oath in a criminal trial."

"You took the money—"

"Because I was scared," Jessica said. Her voice was steady. "Not because I was lying. Because I was twenty-four and terrified, and Margaret Carrington could destroy me. Which she tried to do. Which she succeeded in doing."

She looked at the jury. "I took the money because I needed to survive. But that doesn't mean I lied about being raped. It means Margaret Carrington paid me to stay quiet about her son being a rapist."

Sterling tried a few more questions, attempting to make her sound like someone who came forward for money. Someone who regretted her choice. Someone who was lying. But Jessica didn't break. She just kept answering, kept telling the truth.

When she finally stepped down, she looked exhausted, hollowed out. But she'd done it. She'd told the truth.

Amanda testified next. Then Sarah. Same stories. Same pattern. All three women explaining how Margaret knew, how she paid them off, how she protected Tyler for years.

Each time, I watched Margaret. Small cracks. That's all. The way her breathing quickened. The way she shifted in her seat. The way her hand kept going to her throat.

She was breaking. Slowly. Piece by piece. But she still looked composed, still looked innocent, still looked like someone the jury might believe.

On day three, I testified. I woke up at 6 AM, took a shower, and put on the gray suit Linda had helped me pick out. Conservative. Professional. Like I was someone worth believing. I didn't look like that person in the mirror. I looked like someone drowning.

Linda knocked at 7. "You ready?"

"No."

"Me neither."

We went to the courthouse together, walked through the metal detectors, up the stairs, and into that huge courtroom. The gallery was packed. More people than any other day. Everyone wanted to see Margaret's accuser testify.

I sat in the gallery and waited. Watched people file in. Watched the jury enter. Watched Margaret walk in with her lawyers. She saw me and smiled, small and private, like we shared a secret.

At 9:15, Vanessa stood. "The United States calls Olivia Parker."

My legs moved. Somehow. Up the aisle, through the little gate, to the witness stand. The bailiff held out a Bible. "Raise your right hand."

I did.

"Do you solemnly swear to tell the truth, the whole truth, and nothing but the truth, so help you God?"

"I do." I sat down. The microphone was too close. I could hear my own breathing amplified. Too loud. Too fast. The jury stared at me. Twelve faces. Some curious. Some skeptical. Some already decided.

Vanessa walked toward me. "Ms. Parker, can you state your name for the record?"

"Olivia Parker."

"And how old are you?"

"Twenty-eight."

"Where do you live?"

"Millfield, Ohio." My voice sounded wrong. Too high. Too shaky. I cleared my throat and tried again.

"Ms. Parker, do you have a brother named Leo Parker?"

"I did. He's dead."

"When did he die?"

"April 18, 2014."

"How old was he?"

"Nineteen."

"Can you tell the jury what happened?"

I took a breath and looked at the jury.

"Leo was homeless. He had a drug addiction. Heroin. He'd been on the streets for about two years."

"Why was he homeless?"

"Because our dad died when Leo was seventeen. He started using alcohol and drugs, couldn't hold down a job, and eventually couldn't pay rent."

"Did you help him?"

The question stopped me. "Sometimes. When I could."

"What about in April 2014?"

"He called me three days before he died."

The courtroom was silent, everyone waiting.

"Did he ask for money?"

"Yes. Eight thousand dollars to pay off a debt. He said if he didn't pay, they'd kill him."

"Did you have eight thousand dollars?"

"Yes." Tears were on my face now. "I had more than eight thousand dollars in my checking account. I could have sent it. I chose not to."

"Why?"

"Because I was tired. Tired of enabling him, tired of throwing money at a problem that never got better. I thought I was helping him by saying no. I thought—" My voice broke. "I thought he was manipulating me. I was wrong."

I wiped my face. "So I said no. And three days later, they found him behind a warehouse, shot in the back of the head. Executed."

The jury was watching me. Some sympathetic. Some uncomfortable. All judging.

Vanessa walked to the evidence table and pulled up a photo. "Do you recognize this location?"

"Yes. Club Vertical. Where Leo witnessed a murder that got him killed."

"And who owns Club Vertical?"

"Carrington Media. Margaret Carrington's company."

"Did you know that at the time?"

"No. I didn't learn that until years later when I started researching why my brother died."

"Why did you research Carrington Media?"

"Because I wanted to understand how my brother died, why he died, and who was responsible."

"And what did you learn?"

"That Margaret Carrington's company laundered money for the gang that killed Leo, that they'd been doing it for years, that Margaret knew, that she personally authorized the transactions, and that Leo witnessed one of their murders, and she had him killed to protect herself."

"Objection!" Sterling was on his feet. "Speculation. Move to strike."

"The defendant's signature is on the authorization forms," Vanessa said calmly.

"Overruled. I'll allow it."

Vanessa kept going, walking me through everything. The research. The discovery of fraud, the stock purchase, the proxy fight, Margaret's threats, Steve's evidence.

Forty-five minutes. That's how long it took to tell Leo's story. To explain why his death mattered. Why Margaret needed to pay for it. When Vanessa sat down, I felt empty. Hollowed out. But also clear. I'd told the truth. All of it.

Then Sterling stood. He buttoned his jacket and smiled at me. That same cold smile Margaret used. "Ms. Parker, you testified that you're an alcoholic, correct?"

"I was an alcoholic, but I've been sober for four years."

"But you started drinking after your brother died?"

"Yes."

"Why?"

"To cope with the guilt. The pain. Everything."

"So you blame yourself for Leo's death."

My throat closed. "I did blame myself for years. But I know now—"

"Please answer the question. Do you blame yourself?"

"That's not a fair—"

"It's a yes or no question, Ms. Parker."

I gripped the armrest. "Yes. I blame myself for not answering his calls. But I also blame Margaret Carrington for ordering his murder."

Sterling's smile widened. "You had the money to save him and chose not to send it."

"I had money I could have sent, yes. But he didn't need eight thousand dollars. He needed—"

"Yes or no, Ms. Parker. You had the money. You chose not to send it."

"Yes, but—"

"Thank you. And now you're testifying here because you need someone else to blame. Someone other than yourself."

"That's not true—" I sat forward.

"You're sitting in this witness box blaming Margaret Carrington for your brother's death when the truth is—"

"No. That's not—" I tried to interrupt, but Sterling kept talking, his voice rising over mine. "—you're the one who let him die."

"Objection!" Vanessa stood. "Argumentative and badgering the witness."

"Sustained. Mr. Sterling, let the witness answer."

But the damage was done. The jury had heard it. And Sterling knew it. He smiled. "Let me ask a different question. You purchased ten percent of Carrington Media stock, correct?"

"Yes."

"For how much money?"

"Ten million dollars total. Five and a half million in cash and five million borrowed."

"That's a lot of money for someone who couldn't spare eight thousand for her brother."

My face burned. "That was six years later. I had—"

"Six years. Yes. And where did this fortune come from?"

"I earned it. I built a business—"

"But let's trace the source, shall we?" Sterling walked closer. "You received two million dollars from my client as part of a settlement agreement, correct?"

"A settlement that included an NDA forcing me to stay silent about Tyler Carrington raping me. That's not generosity. That's—"

"Please answer the question. You received two million dollars. Yes or no?"

I clenched my jaw. "Yes."

"And what did you do with that money?"

"I invested part of it. Used some to start a business helping families with children in the NICU. Used the rest to—"

"But most importantly," Sterling cut me off, "you discovered what you claim was fraud at Carrington Media, correct?"

"I discovered actual fraud. Not claimed fraud. Real fraud. Fake subscriber numbers. Revenue manipulation. Securities violations. And I have—"

"Ms. Parker, please just answer the question asked."

"I am answering—"

The judge's voice. "Ms. Parker. Please confine your answers to the specific question."

I looked at the judge. At Sterling. At the system working exactly how Margaret wanted it to.

"Yes," I said through gritted teeth. "I discovered fraud."

"And you sent this information to Blackwood Research, a short-selling firm?"

"I sent it to a research firm that investigates fraud. Yes."

"Knowing they would publish a report that would destroy the stock price?"

"Knowing they would publish the truth. The stock price dropped because the fraud was real, not because—"

"Ms. Parker, yes or no. You knew the report would hurt the stock?"

"Yes, but that's not why—"

"Thank you. And before they published, you shorted Carrington Media stock. You bet against the company. You used two million dollars of settlement money to make that bet."

"I made an investment based on financial analysis—"

"How much did you make when the stock collapsed?"

My throat was tight. "Two point three million dollars."

"Two point three million." Sterling turned to the jury. "So the settlement money from my client became five and a half million dollars because you profited from destroying this family's company."

"I profited from exposing fraud. There's a difference—"

Sterling talked over me. "And then what did you do?"

"I bought stock in the company because the underlying business was sound. The fraud didn't change—"

"How much stock?"

"Ten point two percent—"

"Using how much money?"

"Five and a half million in cash, five million borrowed—"

"You borrowed five million dollars?" Sterling's voice rose. "Took out a loan to buy more of a company you'd just helped destroy?"

"The company was undervalued after the fraud was exposed. The business itself was profitable. I believed—"

"Or you wanted power. You wanted control." Sterling stepped closer. "You wanted to walk into boardrooms and vote against Tyler Carrington. Against this family."

"I wanted accountability—"

"You took your rape settlement, turned it into millions by shorting the family's company, then borrowed even more money to buy voting power so you could destroy them from the inside."

"That's not—" I leaned forward. "That's a complete distortion of—"

"Ms. Parker, please don't interrupt counsel."

I looked at the judge. "Your Honor, he's twisting everything—"

"Ms. Parker. You'll have a chance to respond when he finishes his question."

Sterling smiled. He knew he'd won this round. "That's not seeking justice, Ms. Parker. That's a calculated campaign of financial warfare disguised as activism."

"No. I discovered real fraud. I exposed it. I invested based on—"

"You've spent years weaponizing money against this family."

"I've spent years holding them accountable for crimes—"

"And now you're testifying here, pretending this is about
your brother—"

"It is about my brother—"

"—when really it's about revenge."

"It's about justice!" My voice rose. "Margaret Carrington
ordered Leo's death. She laundered money for the gang that
killed him. She—"

"Ms. Parker." The judge's voice was sharp. "You need to
calm down and wait for the question."

I forced myself to sit back. To breathe. But my whole body
was shaking with rage. Sterling let the silence hang, allowing
the jury to see me angry, emotional, out of control. Then he
continued, quieter now, more dangerous.

"Let's talk about why you're really here. Why you've spent
years and millions of dollars trying to destroy this family."

He turned to me. "Ms. Parker, you are claiming that you
were raped by Tyler Carrington, correct?"

The question hit like a punch. "Yes."

"When?"

"November 2017."

"So you have a personal vendetta against this family."

"I have a right to seek justice—"

"A vendetta that's driven every decision you've made for many years."

"It's not a vendetta. It's—"

"Everything you've done has been motivated by hatred for the Carringtons."

"No. I'm motivated by—"

"Or revenge."

"Justice!" I was shaking. "There's a difference between justice and revenge, and you're—"

"Ms. Parker. Please wait for the actual question," the judge said again.

Sterling smiled. He was winning, and he knew it. "Let's examine your credibility, shall we? You worked as a prostitute, correct?"

My stomach dropped. "Yes. When I was homeless and desperate—"

"For how long?"

"A few months."

"Where?"

"Truck stops outside Chicago."

"That's where you met Tyler Carrington?"

"That's where he found me. Yes."

"He picked you up and paid you for sex, correct?"

"He drugged me and raped me—"

"Or you had consensual sex and regretted it later."

"No!" I sat forward. "That's a lie. He drugged me. He tied me down. He—"

"Ms. Parker—" the judge warned.

"He's calling me a liar!" I looked at the judge. "Your Honor, I have medical records. I have a rape kit. I have—"

"Ms. Parker, you need to answer the questions asked, not make speeches."

I looked at the jury. Some were sympathetic. Some skeptical. But they'd heard Sterling's version. They'd seen me lose control.

Sterling stepped back, looked at Margaret, then back at me. "Ms. Parker, let's be clear about where you were when my client offered you that settlement. You had nothing. You were a prostitute. An alcoholic with no job, no home, and no prospects."

"I was a rape victim—"

"You were selling your body at truck stops to survive."

"Because I was homeless after being raped—"

"And Margaret Carrington offered you two million dollars."

"To stay silent about what her son did—"

"Two million dollars, Ms. Parker." He walked closer. "More money than you'd ever seen in your life. That money gave you everything. A home. A business. A future for your daughter."

"That money was—"

"Everything you have came from Margaret Carrington."

"That's not true!" I was standing now. "Everything I have came from exposing fraud, from building a business, from working—"

"Ms. Parker, sit down, please." The judge's voice was steel.

I sat, shaking, my chest heaving. Sterling let the moment breathe, allowing the jury to see me emotional, unstable. Everything he wanted them to see.

"And yet here you sit. Millions in your bank account. A stake in the family's company. Financial security you never would have had without her generosity." His voice rose. "And you're still filled with hatred. Still trying to destroy them. Still attacking the woman who gave you a second chance at life."

"She gave me hush money!" My voice cracked. "Not a second chance. Money to cover up a rape. That's not—"

"Ms. Parker." The judge leaned forward. "You need to control yourself. Final warning."

I looked at Margaret. I couldn't help it. She was watching me. Steady. Calm. A small smile at the corner of her mouth. That smile said everything. She'd won. Sterling had trapped me, made me look unstable. Vengeful. Everything they wanted.

"Ms. Parker?" Sterling's voice seemed distant. "Do you have a response?"

I gripped the armrest, forcing my voice to be steady. "Yes. I have a response. Every word you just said twisted the truth. Margaret didn't show me generosity. She gave me blood money to cover up what her son did. I didn't weaponize that money. I used it to survive, to build a life. And then I discovered that the same family who raped me was connected to my brother's death. So yes, I fought back. I exposed fraud. I bought stock. I joined shareholder activists. Because that's what you do when powerful people think they're above the law."

Sterling smiled, as if I had just proved his point. "You took her money," he said quietly. "Built your life with it. And then you weaponized it against her. Shorted her company, bought voting shares, joined forces with activists to destroy what she built."

"I joined forces with people seeking accountability—"

"And you expect this jury to believe that a former prostitute with a criminal record—"

"Objection!" Vanessa stood. "Your Honor, this is outrageous—"

"—a recovering alcoholic who let her own brother die—"

"Your Honor!" Vanessa's voice rose.

"—someone who profits from destroying the family that saved her from the streets—"

"Mr. Sterling!" The judge's gavel came down hard. "That's enough. The jury will disregard that last statement." But they couldn't. They'd heard it. All of it.

Sterling turned to face the jury. "This is the woman asking you to believe that a respected philanthropist who gave her everything is responsible for gang violence in Ohio."

"I'm asking them to believe the evidence—" I started.

"Ms. Parker, you are not to speak unless asked a direct question."

I sat back, defeated. Every time I fought back, they shut me down. The judge. Sterling. The whole system working exactly how Margaret wanted it to. Sterling's voice grew quieter, more dangerous. "And you expect this jury to believe you?"

I looked at the jury. At the judge. At Vanessa, who was shaking her head slightly, telling me to stay calm and not give Sterling more ammunition. But I was done being quiet. Done letting him twist everything.

"Yes," I said, my voice shaking but clear. "Because every single thing I said is true. Margaret Carrington ordered my brother's death. The evidence proves it. Steve Adler's testimony proves it. The bank records prove it. The video proves it. And you can attack me all you want. You can call me every name. You can twist every choice I made. But you can't change the facts. Margaret Carrington is a murderer. And I'm not going to sit here quietly while you pretend otherwise."

The courtroom went silent. Sterling smiled. "No further questions."

I stood. My legs barely held me up. The hallway floor tilted as I walked. Linda caught me outside. "You fought like hell in there."

"I couldn't stop him." My voice was shaking. "Every time I tried to explain, they shut me down. Every time I fought back, he twisted it. And the judge... the judge kept warning me to calm down, like I was the problem. Like defending myself made me unstable."

"You weren't unstable. You were fighting back. That's different. You told the truth, even when they tried to silence you." Linda's voice was fierce. "That matters."

I wanted to believe her. But Sterling's words echoed in my head. Margaret's smile burned behind my eyes. I'd fought back, tried to explain, tried to defend myself. And they'd shut me down. Over and over. Until I looked exactly like what Margaret wanted: emotional, vengeful, out of control. Margaret had still smiled. And I didn't know if that meant I'd won something or lost everything.

Chapter Nine

The Verdict

THE TRIAL LASTED TWO more weeks after I testified. I didn't go back. I couldn't bring myself to walk through those courthouse doors. I couldn't sit in that gallery watching more witnesses while Sterling's voice echoed in my head.

You had nothing. She gave you everything.

Linda wanted me there. She said the jury needed to see the victims. See us alive. See what Margaret had tried to destroy. But I stayed in the hotel room. Curtains drawn. TV off. Just me and the silence.

Day seventeen. Closing arguments. Linda drove us to the courthouse. Neither of us spoke. What was there to say? We sat in the back row. I kept my head down. Baseball cap pulled low. I didn't want anyone looking at me. I didn't want to be seen.

The courtroom was packed. Standing room only. Everyone wanted to see how the story ended. Margaret sat at the defense table in her orange jumpsuit. Back straight. Hands folded. Like she was in a board meeting instead of on trial for murder.

Vanessa stood. She walked to the jury box. Navy suit. Hair pulled back. She looked exhausted. We all looked exhausted. "For seven years, Margaret Carrington got away with it." Her voice was steady. Strong. "She built an empire while people died. She laundered money for gangs that executed witnesses. She paid for Leo Parker's murder. She ordered David Keller killed three days before he could testify."

She paused. Looked at each juror. "Leo Parker was nineteen years old. He saw something at Club Vertical he shouldn't have seen. And Margaret Carrington made sure he never got the chance to tell anyone. She paid the gang. She authorized the transaction. She signed off on his death."

Vanessa's voice grew quieter. More dangerous.

"Don't let her walk out of here. Don't let another mother get that phone call. Don't let another witness die for telling the truth." She sat down.

Sterling stood. Buttoned his jacket. Smiled at the jury like they were old friends. "Ladies and gentlemen." His voice was warm. Reasonable. "The prosecution wants you to believe in conspiracies. They want you to trust criminals cutting deals to save themselves. People with axes to grind. People consumed by guilt."

He walked toward the jury. "Steve Adler is a confessed fraudster. He lied for twelve years. Why believe him now? Because he says he's telling the truth *this* time?"

He paused. Let it sink in. "And Olivia Parker." He gestured toward the back of the courtroom. Toward me. "A woman who let her brother die when she had the money to save him. Now she's desperately looking for someone else to blame. Someone to make her feel less responsible for that phone call she didn't answer."

I couldn't breathe. Everyone was looking. Turning in their seats. Staring. Linda grabbed my hand. Squeezed hard.

Sterling kept going. "Margaret Carrington is a successful businesswoman. She's made enemies. That doesn't make her a murderer. That makes her successful."

He walked back to the defense table and stood behind Margaret, protective. "Don't convict someone based on guilt and conspiracy theories. Require proof. Real proof. Not stories people tell themselves to sleep at night." He sat down.

The judge gave instructions: forty minutes of legal language about reasonable doubt, burden of proof, and standards of evidence. Then, "The jury will now deliberate."

They filed out: twelve people who would decide if Leo's death mattered, if his life had been worth something, if anyone cared that a nineteen-year-old kid died begging for his sister to save him. The courtroom emptied.

Day one of deliberations. Nothing. Linda and I sat in the courthouse hallway from 8 AM to 6 PM. Other people came and went: victims' families, reporters, lawyers. I saw Jessica. She nodded at me. Small. Sad. We didn't speak.

Day two. Still nothing. I went to the bathroom around 2 PM. I just needed to move, to not be sitting in that hallway anymore. Jessica was at the sink when I walked in, washing her hands. She looked up when she saw me in the mirror. "Hey," she said.

"Hey." I went into a stall. Didn't really needed to use it, just somewhere to be that wasn't that hallway.

When I came out, Jessica was still there, drying her hands and taking her time. "You doing okay?" she asked.

"Not really. You?"

"Same." She threw the paper towel away. "Listen. A few of us have been talking about what happens after. You know, after the verdict. Whatever it is."

My stomach tightened. "Talking about what?"

"Just... options. Ways to make sure Margaret and Tyler actually face consequences even if the legal system fails us." She looked at me directly. "I can't say more right now. But you should know you're not alone in this. None of us are."

"Who's us?"

"I'll reach out after this is done, after we know what the jury decides." She touched my arm briefly. "Just... don't make any big decisions about Tyler without talking to some people first. Okay?"

"What people?"

"People who understand. People who have resources." She headed for the door, then stopped. "Noreen Keller's been asking about you. You should talk to her."

"Keller's daughter?"

"Yeah. She inherited a lot when Margaret killed her father. And she's been waiting for the right moment." Jessica pushed open the door. "Just don't give up yet, even if today feels hopeless." Then, she was gone.

I stood there, hands wet, heart pounding. Noreen Keller. Other victims. Resources. Options. What the hell did that mean? Linda found me in the bathroom five minutes later. "You okay?"

"Yeah. Just... Jessica said something weird."

"What?"

"That people have been talking about options, about making sure Tyler faces consequences."

Linda's face went careful. "What kind of options?"

"I don't know. She wouldn't say." I dried my hands. "But she mentioned Noreen Keller. Said she has resources."

"Keller's daughter inherited Titan Capital. That's not just resources. That's billions."

We looked at each other. "You think they're planning something?" I asked.

"I think victims don't usually organize quietly unless they're planning something big." Linda held the door open. "Come on. Let's get back."

But I couldn't stop thinking about it. Jessica's face. The way she said "you're not alone." The way she mentioned Noreen specifically. Something was happening. Something bigger than just waiting for a verdict. And I didn't know if that made me feel better or more terrified.

Day three. 4:37 PM. My phone buzzed. Vanessa.

Jury has a verdict.

The words stopped my heart. We ran down the hallway, through security, up the stairs, and burst through the courtroom doors. The gallery was already packed. Word spread fast. Everyone wanted to see the end.

We found seats in the middle, fifth row. I needed to see Margaret's face. Needed to see what happened when everything came down. Margaret walked in with Sterling and her legal team. Orange jumpsuit. Handcuffs. But her back was straight. Her face calm. She sat at the defense table like she owned it. I saw Jessica across the aisle. Amanda beside her. Sarah two rows back. All of us watching. All of us waiting to see if Margaret would finally pay.

The jury filed in. None of them looked at Margaret. That's supposed to mean guilty. But I'd learned not to trust supposed-to-means. My heart hammered. Too fast. Too hard. Linda grabbed my hand.

The judge entered. Everyone stood. Sat. The rustling of bodies settling. Breathing. Waiting.

"I understand the jury has reached a verdict?"

The forewoman stood. Black woman. Mid-fifties. Teacher. I remembered her face from jury selection. Remembered wondering what she thought of me. If she believed me. If she blamed me.

"We have, Your Honor."

The silence stretched. Impossible. Everything balanced on the next words. My whole body was shaking. I couldn't stop it. Couldn't control it. Seven years. Everything. All of it coming down to what happened next.

"Will the defendant please rise?"

Margaret stood. Sterling beside her. Her hands were steady on the table. But I saw the tension in her shoulders. The way her jaw clenched. She was afraid. Finally. Really afraid.

"On count one, RICO violations, how do you find?"

The forewoman looked at Margaret. Held her gaze. The silence stretched. Infinite. The air too thick to breathe.

"Guilty."

The word exploded through the courtroom. Someone gasped behind me. A reporter's pen scratched frantically. Someone whispered, "oh my God."

Linda's hand crushed mine. I couldn't feel my fingers. Margaret didn't move. Didn't react. Just stood there. But I saw her hand twitch. Just once. Saw the crack forming.

"On count two, money laundering, how do you find?"

"Guilty."

My chest was so tight I couldn't breathe. The room tilted. Linda's hand was the only thing keeping me here.

"On count three, conspiracy to obstruct justice, how do you find?"

"Guilty."

Sterling was writing fast. Desperate. His friendly mask cracking.

"On count four, conspiracy in the murder of David Keller, how do you find?"

The forewoman looked at the paper. At Margaret. Back to the paper.

"Guilty."

Margaret's knuckles went white as she gripped the table. I saw her breath catch. I saw the perfect control fracturing. They kept reading.

Count five: Guilty.

Count six: Guilty.

Count seven: Guilty.

Each word was a hammer. Each verdict a door slamming shut on Margaret's perfect life. I lost count. I stopped listening to the numbers. I just heard the word over and over.

Guilty. Guilty. Guilty. Like a heartbeat. Like Leo's name. Like the phone calls I didn't answer.

Margaret stood frozen. Not moving. Barely breathing. Her perfect posture was the only thing holding her together. Then, the forewoman looked down at her paper. Paused. Looked up at the judge.

"On count twelve, first-degree murder in the death of Leo Parker, how do you find?"

Everything stopped.

The courtroom held its breath. The air went still. No one moved. No one breathed. This was it. Leo. My brother. The reason for everything. The reason I'd borrowed millions. The reason I'd spent seven years chasing ghosts. The reason I was here.

The forewoman looked at Margaret. Then at me. Then back at the paper in her hand.

"Not guilty."

The words didn't make sense at first.

Not guilty. On Leo.

Not guilty.

My brain couldn't process it. Couldn't understand. I heard the words, but they didn't connect to meaning.

Not guilty. For murdering Leo.

Not guilty. The room tilted. The floor dropped away. My vision went white at the edges. I couldn't breathe. Couldn't think. Couldn't hear anything except those two words echoing in my skull like a scream.

Not guilty. Not guilty. Not guilty.

Linda was saying something. Her mouth was moving. But I couldn't hear her. Couldn't hear anything except Leo's voice before he died. *Please, Livvy. They're going to kill me. Please. I need eight thousand dollars. Please.* And I'd said no.

The forewoman kept reading. More counts. More verdicts. Her voice seemed to come from underwater. From far away.

"On count thirteen, conspiracy to commit murder related to the death of Leo Parker, we find the defendant guilty."

Guilty on conspiracy. Not guilty on murder.

They believed Margaret was involved. They believed she conspired. But they couldn't prove she directly ordered Leo's death. The timeline was too loose and old. The evidence too circumstantial. Margaret paid the gang on April 19th. Leo died on April 18th. But they couldn't connect them definitively.

So guilty on conspiracy. But not murder. Which meant what? That Leo's death was still just a drug deal gone wrong? That my brother was still just a junkie who got himself killed? That nobody murdered him? That I'd spent seven years, borrowed millions, and destroyed my relationship with Grace to prove something that didn't matter?

More verdicts. More guilty counts. Racketeering. Obstruction. Money laundering. Conspiracy in Keller's death. But not Leo. Not the thing that mattered. Not the reason I was here.

The judge thanked the jury, set sentencing for two weeks, and dismissed them. The courtroom erupted, reporters rushing out, people talking and moving. Chaos.

I sat frozen. Couldn't move. Couldn't think. "Olivia." Linda's voice seemed far away. "Olivia, we won. She's going to prison. We won." But it didn't feel like winning. It felt like I'd lost everything.

Outside, the February air hit my face. Cold. Sharp. Real. I stood on the courthouse steps and couldn't remember how to walk.

Vanessa found us. "I know the murder charge wasn't what you wanted. But guilty on RICO with multiple deaths means life. Twenty-five to thirty years minimum. Margaret will die in prison either way."

"But not for Leo." My voice sounded dead. Empty.

"The conspiracy charge covers Leo. She's going to prison for her role in his death. I know it's not murder one, but—"

"She didn't murder him." The words tasted like ash. "That's what the jury said. She conspired. She was involved. But she didn't murder him."

"Olivia—"

"So what was he? Just collateral damage? Just a junkie who got caught in the wrong place? Just another dead addict nobody cares about?"

Vanessa put her hand on my shoulder. "Leo was a victim. The jury believed that. They found her guilty of conspiracy in his death. That matters."

But it didn't matter. Not really. Then, who was really responsible? I couldn't go back to the hotel. Couldn't face those four walls. Couldn't be still.

"Drive me somewhere," I told Linda. "Anywhere. I don't care."

She drove out of Chicago, through suburbs, past strip malls and gas stations. She kept going until the buildings thinned out and fields appeared. She pulled over at a rest stop, empty except for a few trucks. We sat in the parking lot, neither of us speaking.

"Sterling was right," I finally said. My voice was hollow. "I let Leo die."

Linda pulled me into her arms. We sat in that parking lot until the sun set. Until I had no tears left. Finally, she started the car. "Let's go home."

"To the hotel?"

"No. Home. To Millfield. To Grace. You're done. This is done."

"But the sentencing—"

"I don't care. You're done. Grace needs you. I need you. The dead don't need anything. The living need you here."

We drove straight through. Three hours. Linda wouldn't stop for anything except gas. I stared out the window at the dark highway, at Ohio spreading out around us. Flat fields. Empty sky. Home.

"You should sleep," Linda said.

"I can't."

"Try."

But I couldn't sleep. I couldn't stop seeing Leo's face. I couldn't stop hearing the jury say *not guilty*. She'd go to prison. Twenty-five years at least. She'd die there. But not for killing Leo. For conspiracy. For RICO. For all the other things. Just not for the thing that mattered most.

We pulled into Linda's driveway at 2:47 AM. The house was dark. The nanny texted us that Grace was asleep inside. I sat in the car for a long time, staring at the house, at the life I'd nearly destroyed chasing ghosts.

"Come on." Linda opened her door. "Let's go inside."

I followed her in, kicked off my shoes, and walked to Grace's room. She was asleep in her bed, a stuffed bunny tucked under her arm, her face peaceful and trusting. I sat on the edge of her bed, just watching her breathe, watching her chest rise and fall. This was real. This mattered. Not verdicts. Not proving Margaret guilty. This child. This heartbeat. This life I'd been given.

Grace stirred and opened her eyes. "Mama?" Her voice was sleepy and confused, like she wasn't sure I was real.

"Hi, baby. I'm home."

She reached for me. I lay down next to her, held her against my chest, and felt her relax into sleep. And sitting there in the dark holding my daughter, I finally understood.

Sterling was right about one thing. I'd spent seven years looking for someone to blame, someone to make responsible, someone to punish. But Leo was still dead. And no verdict would bring him back. No sentence would undo that phone call. No justice would make him nineteen years old again. The dead don't need justice. The living need you here. Time to keep my promises. Time to choose the living.

Grace mumbled something in her sleep and held her bunny tighter. "I'm done, baby," I whispered. "I'm staying. Promise." And this time, I really meant it.

The sentencing was two weeks later. I didn't go. Linda offered to come with me. Vanessa called, saying I should be there, that the judge might ask for victim impact statements. But I stayed home with Grace, made her pancakes for breakfast, walked her to preschool, picked her up afterward, and played blocks on the living room floor. Normal things. Small things. Things that mattered.

Vanessa called at 3:47 PM. "It's done. Twenty-five years. Margaret will be eighty-seven when she gets out, if she gets out."

"Okay."

"Olivia—"

"Thank you for everything. I really mean it."

"I wish we could've gotten murder one."

"Me too. But it's done. It's over. And I need to be done too."

After we hung up, I sat on the couch. Grace was coloring at the coffee table, her tongue sticking out in concentration. Margaret Carrington would die in federal prison. Twenty-five years for all the damage she'd done, just not for murdering Leo. Either way, it was done.

Grace looked up from her coloring. "Mama, you okay?"

"Yeah, baby. I'm okay."

"You look sad."

"I am a little sad, but I'm also happy."

"Why?"

"Because I get to be here with you. And that's the most important thing."

She smiled and went back to coloring. I watched her. This child. This miracle. This life that almost slipped away while I chased ghosts. Not anymore. The dead could rest now. The living needed me here. And finally, after seven years, I was choosing the right path.

Chapter Ten

The Third Option

TYLER'S SENTENCING WAS TWO weeks after Margaret's, at the same federal courthouse in Chicago. Different judge, same cold courtroom that smelled like floor polish and fear.

I sat in the back row with Linda, watching Tyler stand at the defendant's table in his expensive suit. His hair was perfect, his posture perfect. Everything about him screamed innocence, except the facts.

The prosecutor read the charges out loud: "Securities fraud, obstruction of justice, conspiracy to defraud investors. Between 2017 and 2019, Mr. Carrington knowingly misrepresented subscriber numbers and revenue to inflate company valuation. He created fake accounts, manipulated data, and lied to auditors and investors. When discovered, he destroyed evidence and coached employees to lie under oath."

Every word true, every word proven. The fake subscriber numbers that made me think Carrington Media was worth investing in, the revenue manipulation that made my 10% stake look valuable, all of it lies, all of it documented.

Tyler's lawyer stood up, a young guy in a sharp suit with a voice like he'd practiced this speech in front of a mirror.

"Your Honor, my client was under immense pressure from his mother. Margaret Carrington controlled every aspect of this company and demanded results Tyler couldn't deliver honestly. He made mistakes, yes, but he was essentially a victim of her manipulation. He deserves leniency."

The same defense they tried for Margaret: blame someone else, claim victimhood, act like power and money somehow made you helpless.

The judge wasn't buying it. "Mr. Carrington, you are a thirty-two-year-old man with a university education and every advantage in life. Your mother's crimes don't absolve you of yours. You made conscious choices to defraud investors, to destroy evidence, and to lie under oath." She paused and looked at him over her glasses. "This court sentences you to fifteen years in federal prison."

Fifteen years. Tyler's face went white. His lawyer grabbed his arm as if Tyler might collapse. "Your Honor, we request bail pending appeal—"

"Denied. The defendant will be remanded to custody immediately."

Two marshals moved toward Tyler. He looked back at the courtroom. His eyes found mine, not apologetic, not broken, but cold, empty, calculating, as if he was memorizing my face for later. Then they took him away, handcuffs and an orange jumpsuit waiting somewhere, fifteen years in a cell.

I should have felt something: relief, victory, justice. Instead, nothing, like winning a war after everyone you loved had already died on the battlefield.

Linda squeezed my hand. "It's over." But it didn't feel over. It felt like something was starting. We walked out into the October sunlight, a cold wind coming off Lake Michigan. I pulled my coat tighter.

"Grace asked this morning if the bad people are caught," Linda said.

"What did you tell her?"

"I said yes. Was I lying?"

I thought about Margaret in maximum security, about Tyler going to federal prison today.

"No. They're caught."

"So we're safe?" The question hung there, heavy and true.

"We're safer," I said, but it wasn't the same, never the same when people like the Carringtons have money, lawyers, and time.

The call came three days later: emergency bail hearing. Tyler's lawyers had filed an appeal and requested release pending the appeals process.

Vanessa called me at 6 AM. "You should be there. The judge might consider victim impact."

So I went, got on a plane, ninety minutes to Chicago, to the courthouse. Tyler was already there when I walked in, out of the orange jumpsuit and back in his expensive suit, hair perfect again, like the last three days in county jail had never happened.

His lawyer, a different one this time, older, more expensive-looking, stood before the judge. "Your Honor, my client is filing a comprehensive appeal. The process will take eighteen months minimum. Mr. Carrington is not a flight risk. He's lived in Chicago his entire life. His family is here. His daughter is here." That last part aimed at me. "He's willing to post a ten million dollar bond, surrender his passport, wear an ankle monitor, and report weekly to pretrial services."

The prosecutor, not Vanessa, but someone from the federal office, fought back. "He's a convicted felon with unlimited resources and every reason to flee."

The judge thought about it, looked at papers, looked at Tyler.

I wanted to stand up, wanted to scream that he was a rapist, that he was dangerous, that keeping him locked up was the only way Grace stayed safe, but the NDAs, the legal threats, the careful dance we'd done for years... So I stayed silent, hands gripping the bench in front of me, nails digging into wood.

"Bail is granted," the judge finally said. "Ten million dollar bond, ankle monitor, passport surrendered, weekly reporting. If you miss one check-in, Mr. Carrington, you go back inside. Understood?"

"Yes, Your Honor."

Just like that, Tyler walked out of the courtroom a free man. Linda grabbed my arm. "We need to go now."

But Tyler was already looking at me across the courtroom, through the people and the lawyers and the distance. He smiled, small, cold, victorious, then turned and walked away.

"He's coming for you," Linda whispered. I knew; I could feel it like ice in my chest.

The stock had been on a roller coaster. After Margaret and Tyler were both indicted six months ago, the shares crashed hard, dropping from two hundred million to barely eighty million in market cap. Investors fled. Advertisers pulled out. The Carrington name became toxic. But then something unexpected happened.

As the trials concluded and both were convicted, the market started pricing in hope. Hope for new management, hope for a clean slate, hope that without the Carringtons, the company might actually be worth something. The stock climbed back to three hundred million, still down from the pre-fraud peak, but stable, survivable, worth fighting over.

The board meeting was five days later at Carrington Media headquarters in Chicago, on the sixty-second floor. The boardroom was all windows. Chicago spread out below like we owned it, and a conference table could seat twenty. Eight board members were already there when I arrived, talking in low voices and going quiet when they saw me.

Harrison, the former Goldman Sachs guy with gray hair and cold eyes, nodded at me. "Olivia."

"Harrison."

"Quite a week."

"Yeah."

Tyler arrived ten minutes later, ankle monitor hidden under perfectly tailored pants, moving like he owned the building, like the last week had never happened. He sat at the head of the table, didn't ask, just took it.

"Thank you all for coming." His voice was calm and professional, like we were discussing quarterly earnings instead of his criminal conviction. "I know my legal situation has created uncertainty about this company's future. I'm here to resolve that."

One of the board members, Patricia, former CNN executive, leaned forward. "You're a convicted felon, Tyler. How exactly do you plan to run this company?"

"I don't." Tyler pulled out a folder and passed copies around the table. "I'm proposing we bring in professional management, someone with media experience and no connection to the family name, someone who can restore investor confidence."

I opened the folder: resume, references, salary requirements. Marcus Webb, fifty-two years old, twenty years running digital media companies, most recently president of Bloomberg Media, and before that, senior VP at Thomson Reuters. Princeton undergrad, Wharton MBA. Built three profitable media companies from scratch. The credentials were impressive, but the timing was suspicious.

"You want to install a puppet CEO while you pull the strings," I said.

Tyler looked at me with those empty eyes. "Marcus Webb is nobody's puppet. But yes, I retain voting control. I own forty percent of this company: twenty percent mine and twenty percent my mother's that I control through power of attorney. The question isn't whether I have power. It's whether this board wants professional leadership or continued chaos."

"Chaos meaning what?" Harrison asked.

"Meaning the SEC investigation isn't over, meaning our stock price is down thirty percent, meaning we've lost eight major advertisers and our subscriber numbers are dropping." Tyler leaned forward. "Marcus can stabilize this. He has relationships with advertisers, credibility with investors. He can rebuild what my mother destroyed."

"And what do you get?" I asked.

"I get to save this company, keep eight thousand people employed, preserve something my family built over three decades."

Patricia looked at me. "What's your position on this, Olivia?"

Everyone turned, because my 10% was the swing vote. Four board members thought Tyler's plan made sense, and four thought putting a convicted felon in control, even indirectly, was insane.

I was the deciding vote. "I need time to think about it."

"The vote is Monday," Tyler said. "Nine AM. I need your answer by then."

"And if I vote no?"

Tyler's smile was ice. "Then I vote to liquidate. Sell off everything. Distribute the cash to shareholders. Your 10% becomes maybe thirty million dollars. Then we're done. Company gone. Eight thousand jobs gone."

Harrison frowned. "You'd destroy the company out of spite?"

"I'd destroy it to prevent it from being stolen." Tyler looked directly at me. "There are people who want to take this company from my family, who think my legal troubles make us vulnerable. I won't let that happen. So either we vote for professional management and stability, or we vote to end it completely. Those are the options."

He stood up. "Think carefully, Olivia. You have until Monday morning, but remember, eight thousand people's lives are on the line." Then he walked out. The room stayed quiet for a long time. Finally, Harrison spoke. "Well, that was clear."

"He's blackmailing her," Patricia said.

"He's giving her a choice. Take the deal or burn it down." Harrison looked at me. "What are you going to do?"

I didn't know, couldn't think, could only feel Tyler's words echoing in my head.

Eight thousand people's lives are on the line. Using innocent people to manipulate me.

"I'll let you know by Monday," I said. Then I got up and left before anyone could see my hands shaking.

I should have flown home that afternoon, should have gone straight back to Grace, held her, been present, been the mother she needed. Instead, I sat in a hotel room staring at Marcus Webb's resume, at Tyler's proposal, at the impossible choice.

Vote yes: Tyler keeps control, puts his guy in charge. I become complicit in letting a rapist run a billion-dollar company.

Vote no: The company liquidates. Eight thousand innocent people will lose their jobs. My 10% becomes cash but everything I fought for is gone. Both options made me sick.

I booked the last flight home, landed in Cleveland at 11 PM, and drove through dark roads to Linda's house. All the lights were off except the porch.

My phone buzzed. Unknown number. I let it go to voicemail. Thirty seconds later, it buzzed again. Linda looked at me from the kitchen. "You should answer it."

I picked up. "Hello?"

"Olivia Parker?" A woman's voice, familiar but I couldn't place it.

"Yes?"

"This is Jessica Ramirez. I don't know if you remember me—"

I remembered. Tyler's first victim. The Northwestern student, the one who came forward after me. "I remember."

"I'm calling because I've been following the news, Tyler's bail, the board situation." She paused. "I'm calling because there's something you should know, something that might change your decision."

"What?"

"Not on the phone. Can you do a video call today? There are some people I want you to meet."

"Who?"

"Women Tyler hurt and who've been talking, planning, waiting for the right moment." Jessica's voice softened. "You're not alone in this, Olivia. You never were. We just needed you to know we existed."

My chest got tight. "How many?"

"On the call? Four. But more are involved. We've been organizing since the trials, since we watched them both get convicted and realized, what happens to all that power they built? Does it just disappear, or do we take it?"

"Take it how?"

"Video call. One hour. Can you do noon?"

I looked at Grace, at Linda, at the life I was about to lose if I chose wrong. "Yeah, I can do noon."

The video call started at exactly twelve o'clock. Grace was down for her nap. Linda had taken her upstairs. The house was quiet. I sat at the kitchen table with my laptop and clicked the link Jessica had sent.

Four faces appeared on screen.

Jessica Ramirez, thirty-two years old now, sharp eyes, tired but determined. Tyler's Northwestern classmate who he drugged at a fraternity party. The third woman to come forward after me. The one who'd heard Tyler's line: "You don't remember? Wow, you really can't handle your alcohol."

Amanda Lopez, twenty-nine, Northeastern, long dark hair, living in Seattle now, working in tech. The second victim to come forward. The one Tyler drugged after inviting her to dinner, wine at his apartment, when she was twenty-one and he'd already graduated.

Sarah Mitchell, twenty-eight, Boston College, round glasses, professional, working as a paralegal in Portland. The third to come forward. The one whose roommate told her maybe they'd both just drunk too much, so she stayed quiet for years.

And Noreen Keller. I hadn't expected her. Keller's daughter. The woman who inherited Titan Capital when Margaret had her father murdered.

"Thank you for joining us," Jessica said. "I know this is unexpected."

"Why are you calling me?" I asked, direct, no politeness.

"Because Tyler's trying to back you into a corner," Amanda said. "Vote for him or lose everything. That's his play. We want you to know there's a third option."

"Which is?"

"We buy Carrington Media," Sarah said, "All of us, together, and transform it into something that actually matters."

I stared at the screen, waiting for the punchline. "Are you serious?"

"Completely," Noreen said. She leaned forward, her father's eyes, his intensity. "I inherited a lot of money when Margaret killed my father, eighty million dollars in liquid assets. I've been waiting for the right opportunity to honor what he started. This is it."

"You want to buy a three-hundred-million-dollar company with eighty in cash?"

"We've raised more," Jessica said. "Private investors, women's groups, impact funds, people who care about accountability journalism. We're at one hundred and twenty million now and should hit one-fifty by next week."

"That's still half what you need."

"We don't need to buy the whole company," Amanda explained. "We need forty-one percent, controlling interest. Tyler has forty, you have ten. The rest is split among small shareholders. If we buy Tyler out plus pick up eleven percent from others, we control it."

"Tyler won't sell."

"We haven't offered yet," Sarah said. "That's where Monday's vote comes in. Here's the sequence: Vote no on Tyler's CEO proposal. That kills his plan and signals you're with us. Then we make our move."

She pulled up a document. "We offer Tyler 120 million cash for his forty percent. A clean exit before he goes to prison. If he takes it, we combine his forty with your ten, buy another eleven percent from small shareholders, and we control the company, done in thirty days."

"And if he refuses the buyout?"

"Then we launch a proxy fight, campaigning for shareholder votes over six to eight weeks. We'll make the case that a convicted felon shouldn't control a media company, and we'll win. The institutional investors will back us, but it's messier and takes longer."

"So Monday's vote starts everything."

"Exactly. Vote no, signaling you're joining us. Then we approach Tyler with the buyout offer. Either way, buyout or proxy fight, we're taking control. The only question is whether Tyler walks away with 120 million or loses everything fighting us."

"A proxy fight?"

"We campaign for shareholder votes, making the case that Tyler's a convicted felon who destroyed value, that we offer better leadership, that the company needs ethics, not Carringtons." Jessica's voice got intense. "It takes six weeks, maybe eight, but we'll win. The institutional investors will side with us, and the ethical investors will side with us. Tyler will lose."

My head was spinning. "And what do I get?"

"You keep your ten percent," Noreen said. "Join our board. Help us transform this company. No cash payout. You stay invested, but you'll have real power to shape its future."

"What future?"

"Investigative journalism," Amanda said, "exposing corruption, amplifying survivor stories, holding power accountable instead of protecting it." She paused. "We're going to turn Margaret's empire into something that hunts people like her."

"Using their own money," Sarah added, "their own infrastructure. Everything they built to cover up crimes, we'll use to expose them."

I thought about Leo, about the gang that killed him, about all the corruption that Margaret's company helped hide.

"You want to make it mean something."

"We want to make it matter," Jessica said. "Your brother died because powerful people protected criminals. We're going to build a company that does the opposite, that tells those stories, that makes sure no one else's brother dies in the dark."

My throat got tight. "What if you lose?"

The women looked at each other, some communication happening without words. "We won't lose," Jessica finally said. "We have better financing, a better message, better everything." She leaned forward. "But I'll be honest: if we lose, you'll be fighting on every front, so you need to decide if you trust us, if you believe four women who've been planning this for six months can beat one man who's going to prison."

I looked at their faces, at their determination, at the shared pain that connected them, connected all of us. "Why now?" I asked. "Why not months ago?"

"Because Tyler wasn't vulnerable months ago," Noreen said. "He was free, powerful, dangerous. But now? Convicted, out on bail pending appeal, desperate. This is when we strike, when he's weak."

"He doesn't seem weak."

"He's terrified," Sarah said. "That's why he's threatening now, why he's pushing for Monday's vote, because he knows if he loses control of this company, he loses everything."

"So what do you want from me?" I asked.

Jessica's voice got soft, honest. "We want you to vote no on Monday, join our coalition, help us fight."

"For six weeks."

"Maybe eight, depending on the vote count."

"Away from Grace."

"Not completely. You'd fly to New York for board meetings, media interviews, investor pitches, but most of it can be remote." Amanda paused. "I'm not going to lie and say it won't be hard. Tyler will fight dirty. The media will attack us. It'll be brutal, but in the end, if we win, you'll have helped transform a billion-dollar company into something good, something your daughter can be proud of."

I thought about that, about Leo's name in articles, about his death meaning something beyond tragedy.

"I need to think about it," I said.

"You have until Monday morning," Noreen said. "But Olivia, you're not alone anymore. That's what we're offering. Not just money, not just a business deal. We're offering solidarity: four women who know exactly what Tyler is, who know exactly what you've survived, who are saying, we're with you, however you choose."

The screen went dark. I sat there staring at my laptop: four women, three hundred million dollars, a plan to take everything Tyler thought was his, and six more weeks away from Grace.

I couldn't make the decision. Thursday afternoon, Thursday night, Friday morning, the choice paralyzed me. Friday night, after Grace was asleep, I went to Leo's room. Linda had kept it exactly the same, shrine-like, creepy but comforting: his bed, his posters, his stuff, photos on the wall. Leo at four, at ten, at fifteen, at nineteen, the progression of a life that ended too soon.

I sat on his bed, springs creaking, everything smelling dusty and old and sad. "I don't know what to do," I whispered to the empty room, to the ghost of my brother. Silence. No ghost, no voice, just me and the dark.

I picked up the photo from his nightstand, the two of us at six and four, backyard, summer, before Dad's drinking got bad, before everything broke. Leo smiling, gap-toothed, trusting. He'd trusted me to protect him, to keep him safe, to answer when he called, and I'd failed, every time, every way, deleted his messages, ignored his calls, let him die thinking no one was coming.

"I can't fail again," I said. "Can't let Tyler destroy other people anymore." But fighting meant leaving, meant more broken promises, meant Grace learning what I learned about Dad: that love is conditional, presence is negotiable, and parents always choose something else.

I put the photo down and looked at Leo's wall, at all the versions of him. The four-year-old catching fireflies, the fourteen-year-old stealing food, the nineteen-year-old running for his life. All of them gone, all of them lost because I chose wrong.

"Tell me what to do," I said to the dark. "Tell me how to save Grace without becoming Dad. Tell me how to fight without losing everything that matters."

The room stayed silent, but in that silence, I knew I'd been asking the wrong question: not, how do I save Grace? But, what kind of world do I want Grace to grow up in?

A world where men like Tyler keep their power because women are too afraid to fight? Where rapists control billion-dollar companies because victims are too broken to take them back? Where my daughter learns that sometimes you just have to live with injustice because fighting costs too much?

Or a world where four women said "enough" and took everything back, where survivors became the powerful ones, where Grace grows up knowing her mother fought, even when it was hard, even when it cost everything?

I stood up and walked out of Leo's room, down the hall. Linda's door was closed, but light showed underneath. I knocked.

"Come in." She was in bed reading, wearing reading glasses and an old t-shirt. The mom I'd always known.

"Can we talk?" I asked.

Linda closed her book and took off her glasses. "You made your decision."

"How do you know?"

"Because you only knock on my door at midnight when you're about to do something that scares you." She patted the bed. "Sit."

I sat, crossed my legs, and felt like a kid again. "Tyler's using other people's jobs to control me," I said. "Vote for him, or thousands of people will lose their jobs. That's the choice."

"And you're going to fight him."

"How did you know?"

Linda smiled, sad but real. "Because you're your father's daughter, and Bob never backed down, not when it mattered, not when he thought he was protecting us."

"Dad destroyed us."

"No, Dad's addiction destroyed us. His fighting. That's what kept us alive when the drinking tried to kill us." Linda took my hand. "You're not him, Olivia. You're sober. You're present. You're making different choices."

"Am I? Because I'm about to leave Grace again, choose another fight over being her mother."

Linda pulled me into a hug. "Go fight, Olivia. I've got Grace. You go finish this."

I called Tyler Saturday morning. Grace was at the playground with Linda. The house was quiet. I sat at the kitchen table with my phone, hands shaking.

Tyler answered on the second ring. "Olivia."

"I'm voting no."

Silence. Long enough that I thought he'd hung up. Then his voice came back, ice cold. "You're making a mistake."

"Probably, but I'm making it anyway."

"Monday morning, when the board votes no and I liquidate everything, remember this moment. Remember that you will destroy eight thousand families' lives with this decision."

"We'll see." I hung up, sat there staring at my phone, waiting for my hands to stop shaking, waiting for my chest to stop screaming, waiting to feel like I'd made the right choice. But all I felt was terrified.

My phone rang at 9 PM. Linda. I was already in Chicago, already at my hotel, already reviewing notes for tomorrow's board meeting.

"Olivia," her voice was shaking.

My stomach dropped. "What's wrong? Is Grace—"

"Grace is fine, but Tyler's here."

"What?"

"Tyler's at my house, standing on the porch. He knocked five minutes ago. I didn't answer, but he's still there, just standing, waiting."

Ice in my veins. "Call the police."

"And say what? He's not breaking in, he's not threatening, he's just standing there."

"He's violating—" I stopped. He wasn't violating anything. No restraining order, no custody agreement. He was legally allowed to be on Linda's porch.

"What do I do?" Linda asked.

"Don't open the door, don't engage, just wait for him to leave."

"He's looking at Grace's window."

The words made me sick. Tyler standing in the dark, staring at the window where my daughter slept, staring at what he thought he owned.

"I'm coming home," I said. "Right now. I'll get the next flight—"

"No," Linda's voice got firm. "You stay there. You vote tomorrow. You fight him the way we planned." She paused. "He wants to scare you. That's why he's here. Don't let him."

"Mom—"

"I've got a baseball bat, I've got locks, I've got 911 ready to dial, and I've got Grace. He's not getting past me." Linda's voice got stronger. "You go to that board meeting tomorrow. You vote no. You start the fight that ends him, and I'll keep Grace safe until you come home."

"Are you sure?"

"I'm sure. Now hang up. I need to watch him."

The line went dead. I stood in my hotel room, sixty-two floors above Chicago, miles away from Grace, from Linda, from everything that mattered.

Tyler was at Linda's house, right now, standing on the porch, staring at Grace's window, and I wasn't there. I grabbed my phone, started to book a flight, started to run, then stopped, because Linda was right. This was Tyler's play: scare me, make me run home, make me miss tomorrow's vote, make me choose Grace over the fight, make me prove I was too weak to do both.

"Fuck you," I whispered to the empty room, to Tyler three states away, to the fear trying to control me. "Fuck you. I'm not running."

I put down my phone, picked up my notes, and started reviewing again. Tomorrow, I'd vote no, start the proxy fight, and begin the war that would end him. And then I'd go home to Grace, home to Linda, home to everything that mattered.

My phone buzzed. Linda: *He's gone. Left after ten minutes. Grace never woke up. We're okay.*

I texted back: *Good. Lock everything. I'll call after the vote.*

Linda: *Go get him.*

I smiled, a small, fierce, determined smile. "Yeah," I said to the empty room. "I'm going to get him." And I meant it.

Chapter Eleven

The Fight

THE WAR STARTED ON a Monday morning. Tyler rejected the women's offer in a statement released at 9:03 AM. Three sentences: cold and final.

"Phoenix Rising Partners' proposal is an insult to my family's legacy. I will not surrender control of Carrington Media to opportunistic activists with no media experience. This matter will be decided by our shareholders, not by a coalition of vengeful women."

Vengeful women. He couldn't even say our names, couldn't acknowledge what he'd done to us. Just vengeful women.

Jessica called at 9:47. "He wants a fight. We'll give him one."

"When does it start?"

"Now. We're filing our proxy materials today. Shareholders vote in six weeks, May 28th. Winner takes control."

Six weeks. Forty-two days. I thought about Grace. Six more weeks of breaking promises. "I'm in," I said.

"Good, because we need you: investor meetings, Bloomberg interview, CNBC Thursday. We're building momentum fast."

The Bloomberg interview was day three: studio in New York, glass walls, cameras everywhere. The host was Emily Chang: sharp, smart, no softballs.

"Olivia Parker, you're part of a coalition trying to take control of Carrington Media from Tyler Carrington, but you're also Tyler's victim. You accused him of rape six years ago. Isn't this just revenge?"

I'd practiced this answer with Amanda for two hours. "It's accountability. Tyler Carrington is a convicted felon going to prison for fifteen years. He committed securities fraud. He lied to investors. He destroyed evidence. Those are facts, not accusations."

"But the rape allegations were settled privately. You took money, signed an NDA."

"I took money because I needed to survive, because I had a three-year-old daughter and no job, and Margaret Carrington was destroying my life." My voice stayed steady and professional. "But I didn't lie about being raped. The NDA covered public statements, not testimony in criminal trials, not proxy fights."

"So this is revenge."

"This is justice. Tyler used his mother's money and power to avoid consequences for years. He committed fraud. He lied under oath. And now he wants shareholders to let him keep running a billion-dollar company while he appeals his conviction?" I looked directly at the camera. "That's not leadership, that's entitlement."

Emily leaned forward. "Phoenix Rising Partners has raised over a hundred million dollars for this proxy fight. Where's that money coming from?"

"Impact investors, women's funds, people who believe media companies should be run by ethical leaders, not convicted felons."

"And if you lose?"

"We won't lose. The fundamentals are clear. Carrington Media needs change. Shareholders know that, and they're ready for it."

"You sound very confident."

"I am."

After the interview, Amanda found me backstage. "You did great, stayed on message, didn't get emotional."

"I wanted to call him a rapist on live TV."

"I know, but you didn't. That's what matters." She checked her phone. "Two hundred thousand Twitter mentions already, mostly positive. Tyler's team is scrambling."

"Good."

"Next up: CNBC tomorrow morning, then investor calls all afternoon. Friday, you're meeting with Vanguard."

"When do I go home?"

Amanda's face changed. "Sunday. You fly back Sunday morning."

Five days. Not two. Not three. Five. I texted Linda: *Sunday. Sorry.*

Her response came immediately: *Grace asked if you're coming to her preschool show Friday. I told her probably not.*

The guilt hit like a fist. *What show?*

Spring concert. She's been practicing for three weeks. She's a flower and has two lines.

Grace. My baby. A flower in a spring concert, practicing for three weeks, and I didn't even know. *I'll be there.*

You're in New York.

I'll fly back Thursday night, be there Friday morning, and fly back to New York Friday afternoon.

Olivia, that's insane.

I'll be there.

I went back to my hotel, forty-second floor, floor-to-ceiling windows, New York spreading out like I owned it. But I didn't own anything. I was just fighting, again, still, always, choosing the fight over Grace, over normalcy, over peace, just like Dad.

The CNBC interview was worse. The host was skeptical, aggressive, and kept pushing the revenge angle. "You shorted Carrington Media stock before the fraud was exposed, made millions, then bought a stake when it crashed. Now you're trying to take over the company. This looks like opportunism."

"I invested because the company was undervalued, because Tyler's fraud had destroyed real value. I saw an opportunity to help fix it."

"Or you saw an opportunity to get rich and get revenge."

"I'm not getting rich. I'm still invested. If the company fails, I lose everything."

"But if Phoenix Rising wins, you and your coalition control a three-hundred-million-dollar company. That sounds pretty profitable."

"It sounds like shareholders voting for better leadership."

He leaned back and smiled, like he'd won. "Tyler Carrington says you're alcoholics, drug addicts, prostitutes, women with grudges trying to destroy a family business."

The words hit like acid. "Tyler Carrington is a fraud. He can call us whatever he wants. The facts don't change."

"But he has a point, doesn't he? Your past is... complicated."

"My past is surviving, surviving Tyler's rape, surviving his mother's money, surviving their attempts to silence me." My hands were shaking. "And yes, I was an alcoholic. I got sober. I rebuilt my life. I'm raising a daughter. I'm fighting to make sure men like Tyler faces consequences."

"By taking his company."

"By letting shareholders decide who they trust more: a convicted felon or four women who've spent six years rebuilding their lives after he destroyed them."

When I walked off set, Jessica was waiting, her face pale. "What?"

"Tyler's team just released a press packet, photos, documents, affidavits."

"About what?"

She handed me her phone. The headline: **"Olivia Parker: From Prostitute to Activist."**

Underneath: photos of me drunk, homeless, getting into cars with men, the photos Margaret's investigator had taken six years ago, the ones used to destroy me in court.

"They released everything," Jessica said quietly. "Your prostitution, your alcoholism, your psych records from the hospital."

I stared at the screen. At my own face. Destroyed. Again. For everyone to see.

"Grace's school will see this."

"I know."

"Her teachers. The other parents."

"I know."

"She'll see it. Eventually. When she's older. She'll google my name and find these photos."

Jessica took the phone back. "Then we make sure she also finds the truth, that you survived, that you fought back, that you won."

"Did I win? Because right now it feels like Tyler's destroying me all over again."

"He's trying, but we're not letting him." She looked at me. "Can you keep going? Can you do tomorrow's investor meetings? Can you keep fighting?"

I thought about Grace, a flower in a spring concert, two lines she'd been practicing. I thought about Leo, calling for help, getting none. I thought about Tyler, smiling in that courtroom, memorizing my face, planning this moment.

"Yeah," I said. "I can keep fighting."

"Good, because we're winning. The polls show it. Shareholders trust us more than him. He's desperate. That's why he's going so dirty."

"What if he wins anyway?"

"He won't. We have the numbers. We have the momentum. We just need to not break."

Not break. Four years sober. Five months fighting. Seven years since Leo died. I'd broken a hundred times. Shattered. Rebuilt. Shattered again. But I was still here, still standing, still fighting. So yeah, I could not break one more time.

I made it to Grace's concert, flew back Thursday night, red-eye, landed in Cleveland at 6:47 AM, drove straight to Linda's house. Grace was still asleep. Linda was making coffee in the kitchen.

"You came."

"I promised."

"You look like hell."

"I feel like it."

Linda poured me coffee and sat down across from me. Her face was hard to read.

"The photos are everywhere. Parents at Grace's school have seen them. Some are asking if Grace should be in a different class."

The words were like knives. "Because of me."

"Because they're scared, because they don't understand, because Tyler's team is very good at making you look dangerous."

"I am dangerous only to him."

"But you're Grace's mother, and she doesn't understand why you're gone all the time, why other kids' parents are whispering about you, why her mama's face is on TV with horrible words underneath."

"Did you tell her?"

"I told her that some people are saying mean things about you because you're fighting bad people, that the bad people are trying to make you look bad so you'll stop fighting."

"What did she say?"

Linda's eyes got wet. "She said, 'Mama always fights bad people.'"

The words broke me. "I can't quit," I whispered. "I'm so close. We're winning."

The concert was in the preschool gymnasium: folding chairs, a makeshift stage, and parents everywhere with phones ready. Grace was in the back with her class: eleven four-year-olds in flower costumes. She saw me in the audience, and her whole face lit up. She waved, almost knocking over the kid next to her.

Some parents near me whispered, and I caught fragments. "That's her."

"The prostitute?"

"Saw the photos online. Horrible."

"Poor child."

I ignored them, kept my eyes on Grace, smiled, and waved back.

The show started. A teacher played piano, and the flowers walked out, swaying and singing about spring. Grace was in the back row, green petals around her face, completely serious and focused. When her part came, she stepped forward, loud and clear: "Spring is here. The flowers grow."

Small pause. "Look at us. We're all in a row."

Then she smiled, huge, looking right at me. I was crying and couldn't help it; I couldn't stop. Linda found my hand and squeezed. "She practiced so hard," Linda whispered, "every single day, for you."

The show ended. Parents clapped, teachers bowed, and the flowers waved. Grace ran to me, still in her costume. "Did you see?"

"You did perfect. You were the best flower."

"Did you see me remember both lines?"

"I saw everything."

She hugged me, then pulled back, and her face got serious. "You have to go now?"

"Yeah, my flight's at three."

"When will you be back?"

"Two more weeks, then I'm home forever."

"Okay." She kissed my cheek. "Love you, Mama."

"Love you too, baby."

Linda took her hand and led her away to change. Grace looked back once, waved, then disappeared into the classroom. And I stood there in that gymnasium, parents still whispering about me, my daughter's kiss still on my cheek, knowing I had two more weeks of this, two more weeks of choosing, of fighting.

The final two weeks were brutal. Tyler's team released more documents, more photos, and audio recordings of me drunk six years ago, rambling incoherently, and saying horrible things about Grace.

The headlines: "**Olivia Parker Called Her Daughter a Mistake.**" It was from a therapy session, one session, one moment of despair when Grace was six months old and I was drowning. But Tyler's team took that one sentence, played it everywhere, and made it sound like I hated my daughter.

Grace's preschool asked Linda to keep her home for a few days, "just until things calm down." Translation: other parents are scared; your daughter is a PR problem.

Jessica called at 2 AM. I was awake and couldn't sleep. "Tyler's proposing a settlement. He'll not nominate the next CEO, accept a board seat, and keep his voting rights. Phoenix Rising gets two board seats, and everything else stays the same."

"What's that mean?"

"It means he keeps control. He doesn't go away; he just pretends to."

"So we lose."

"No. We reject his proposal, keep fighting, and win the vote. But Olivia..." Her voice got soft. "Are you okay, like really okay? Because if you need to step back—"

"I'm fine."

"You don't sound fine."

"I'm two weeks from being done, two weeks from going home to Grace. I just need to make it."

"Okay. But if you can't—"

"I can." I could. I had to, because quitting now meant everything was for nothing. All the damage, all the broken promises, all of it. I had to win, had to make it worth something.

The shareholder meeting was at the Hilton Midtown on Sixth Avenue. I woke up at 4 AM and couldn't go back to sleep, just lay there in the dark hotel room three blocks away, counting my heartbeats. By 6, I'd thrown up twice. Nothing came up the second time.

The meeting started at 10 AM. I got there at 9:15. The ballroom was huge: chandeliers, dark carpet, rows of chairs facing a stage, eight hundred shareholders filing in, reporters lining the back wall, cameras everywhere.

Tyler was already there, standing near the front with his lawyers, perfect suit, perfect hair, talking to shareholders like this was just another business meeting, like he wasn't a convicted felon, like everything was fine.

He saw me. Our eyes met across the ballroom. He smiled, small and cold, like he'd already won. I looked away first, hating myself for it.

Jessica found me near the entrance. "You okay?"

"No."

"Me neither." She was pale, hands shaking. "Amanda's in the bathroom throwing up. Sarah can't stop pacing. Noreen keeps checking her phone like the results are already in."

"What if we lose?"

"We won't."

"But what if we do?"

Jessica grabbed my arm, hard. "Then we lost fighting, but we're not going to lose. Look at this room, Olivia. Eight hundred shareholders showed up in person. That means they care. That means we got their attention."

A man in a Carrington Media staff shirt started directing people to seats: shareholders for Phoenix Rising on the left side of the ballroom, shareholders supporting Tyler on the right, undecided in the middle.

The right side filled up fast. The middle was packed. Our left side had maybe a third of the chairs filled.

My stomach dropped. "Jessica—"

"Institutional investors haven't sat down yet," she said quickly. "Vanguard, BlackRock, Fidelity. They always wait until the last minute."

"What if they vote against us?"

"Then Tyler wins and we start planning an appeal." Her voice was steady, but her hands were shaking. "But they're not going to vote against us. We have a better case."

At 9:47, Tyler walked onto the stage. The right side applauded, loud and long, like he was a hero instead of a criminal. He waved, smiled, looked comfortable up there, like he belonged. Jessica's hand found mine, squeezed hard.

At 9:52, a man in a gray suit took the podium. The moderator. "Good morning. I'll be moderating today's annual shareholder meeting and special vote. We're here to vote on two competing slates of directors for Carrington Media."

He explained the process: how voting would work, paper ballots, counted by an independent firm, results in approximately thirty minutes after voting closed. I barely heard him and just kept staring at Tyler on stage, at how calm he looked.

At 9:58, Vanguard's delegation walked in. Six people in business suits sat in the middle section, undecided.

Jessica's grip on my hand tightened until it hurt. "We need them," she whispered. "Vanguard has 8%. If they vote against us, we lose."

The moderator's voice cut through the room. "Mr. Carrington, you have ten minutes for your opening statement."

Tyler walked to the podium, adjusted the microphone, and looked out at eight hundred faces. "Thank you all for being here. I know many of you traveled far. I know this is an unusual situation." His voice was measured and reasonable. "I'm facing legal challenges. I won't pretend otherwise, but those challenges don't change what this company is, what my family built over thirty years."

He paused and let that land. "Carrington Media has eighty million subscribers, eight thousand employees, and bureaus in forty countries. That's not luck. That's three decades of hard work, of vision, of leadership."

Some shareholders nodded, while others stayed stone-faced.

"Now, a group of activists wants to take that legacy. They're using my legal troubles, which I'm actively appealing, to justify a hostile takeover. They have no media experience, no track record running a company, just grievances and revenge."

I felt sick.

"I'm asking you to look past the personal attacks, past the noise, and ask yourself one question: who do you trust to run this company, someone with thirty years of experience or four women with an agenda?"

The right side erupted in applause. The middle section stayed quiet, and our left side didn't move. Tyler sat down, smiled at his lawyers, confident and certain.

"Ms. Ramirez, you have ten minutes."

Jessica stood and walked to the stage. Her hands were shaking so badly I could see it from my seat. She gripped the podium and looked out at the crowd. "Tyler Carrington just asked you to look past the noise, so let's do that. Let's look at facts."

A slide appeared on the screen behind her: Tyler's conviction details. "Fact one: Tyler Carrington was convicted by a jury of twelve people for securities fraud, obstruction of justice, and conspiracy to defraud investors. That's not a legal challenge. That's a conviction."

Another slide: a stock price chart showing the 97% drop. "Fact two: He lied about subscriber numbers, created fake accounts, and manipulated revenue data, then destroyed evidence when investigators got close."

Another slide: the judge's sentencing remarks. "Fact three: He was sentenced to fifteen years in federal prison." The judge said, quote, "This was a systematic betrayal of shareholder trust."

Her voice was steady now, stronger. "Tyler wants you to trust his experience, but his experience is fraud, his track record is lies, and his legacy is a company that lost 97% of its value because of his crimes."

She stepped away from the podium and looked directly at the crowd. "Phoenix Rising isn't offering experience. We're offering something better: honesty, ethics, accountability. We won't lie to you. We won't commit fraud. We won't destroy evidence when auditors come calling."

A pause. The room was completely silent.

"Tyler said we're women with an agenda. He's right. We do have an agenda." Her voice dropped, became personal. "Our agenda is making sure convicted criminals don't run billion-dollar companies. Our agenda is believing that shareholders deserve better than a CEO who's going to prison."

She looked at Tyler. He stared back, cold. "And yes, we have another agenda too. His mother paid us millions to disappear, and for six years, we stayed silent, took the money, let him keep running this company."

The room was so quiet I could hear my own heartbeat. "But we're not silent anymore. We're not taking money to go away. We're taking this company back, not just for us, but for every shareholder he lied to, for every employee who lost their job when the stock crashed, for everyone who trusted a Carrington and got betrayed."

She walked back to her seat. The left side erupted in a standing ovation. The middle section stayed seated, watching, thinking. The right side didn't move.

Tyler stood for his rebuttal. "May I respond?"

The moderator nodded. Tyler walked to the podium, calm, controlled. "Ms. Ramirez's speech was very emotional, very personal, but emotion doesn't run a company. Experience does." He looked at Vanguard's section. "I'm asking the institutional investors in this room to vote with your heads, not your hearts. This company needs stability, not revenge."

He sat down. The moderator stood. "Thank you both. Shareholders, voting is now open. You have thirty minutes. Ballots are being distributed."

Staff in Carrington Media shirts moved through the rows, handing out paper ballots. Shareholders marked their choices. I couldn't move, just sat there watching. Jessica leaned over. "Olivia, breathe."

"I can't."

"You have to. We have thirty minutes."

Thirty minutes. I looked at my phone: 10:34 AM. The ballots would be counted by 11:04. Half an hour to find out if the last six weeks meant anything. I stood up. "I need air."

"Olivia—" But I was already walking, through the rows, past shareholders filling out ballots, past reporters watching everything. I found the bathroom, locked myself in a stall, put my head between my knees, tried to breathe. The door opened. Someone else came in.

"Olivia?" Amanda's voice.

"I'm here."

"You okay?"

"No. The right side is huge. The middle is packed. We're going to lose."

"We're not going to lose." Amanda's voice was firm. "Vanguard hasn't voted yet, and neither has BlackRock nor Fidelity. That's 22% right there. If they vote for us, we win."

"What if they don't?"

"Then we fight the appeal. But Olivia, look at what we did. We stood up there, in front of eight hundred people, in front of Tyler, and we told the truth. That matters."

"Does it?"

"Yes. Even if we lose, it matters."

I came out of the stall and washed my hands. The water was cold, real. Amanda was leaning against the sink. "I threw up twice this morning."

"Me too."

"Sarah can't stop shaking. Noreen keeps checking her phone like she's going to find the results early." Amanda smiled, small and scared. "We're a mess."

"We are."

"But we're here. We showed up. We fought."

We went back to the ballroom. 10:48 AM. Shareholders were still voting, staff collecting ballots in boxes. Everything was moving in slow motion.

I found my seat. Jessica was texting someone. Sarah was staring at the stage. Noreen was checking her phone. Tyler was talking to his lawyers, laughing and confident.

10:52 AM. Staff started carrying the ballot boxes out to a back room where the counting would happen.

10:56 AM. The moderator took the podium. "Voting is now closed. All ballots are being counted. Results will be announced shortly. Please remain seated."

Shortly. Not thirty minutes. Shortly. How long was shortly? I looked at my phone, tried to do math, started counting seconds. Jessica grabbed my hand. "Stop. You're making it worse."

"How long does counting take?"

"I don't know."

"What if—"

"Stop. Whatever happens, happens. We did everything we could."

I looked at Tyler. He was on his phone, smiling at something, not worried, not scared, just certain he'd won.

11:03 AM. No announcement yet. 11:07 AM. Still nothing. The ballroom was getting restless, shareholders talking, reporters moving around, everyone waiting.

11:12 AM. My hands were shaking so badly I had to sit on them.

11:15 AM. The side door opened. A woman in a business suit walked to the moderator and handed him a folder. He opened it, read it. His face showed nothing. Then he walked to the podium. The room went silent. "Results are final. Here are the numbers."

He put the paper on the podium and looked out at the crowd. "Phoenix Rising Partners slate received 52.3% of the votes."

The words didn't make sense at first. 52.3%. We won. The left side exploded, people screaming, standing, hugging. The right side sat in shocked silence. The middle section started clapping, slow, then faster.

I couldn't move, couldn't breathe, couldn't process. 52 .3%. We actually won.

Jessica grabbed me and pulled me up. She was crying, sobbing. "We did it. We actually did it." Amanda was screaming, actually screaming, hands in the air. Sarah had her hands over her face, shoulders shaking, crying so hard she couldn't stand. Noreen was just staring at the stage, mouth open, in shock.

I looked at Tyler. He was sitting very still, face white, completely frozen. Then he stood up, slowly, like his legs weren't working right. He looked at me across the ballroom, not angry, not defeated, just... empty, like something inside him had broken. His lawyer was talking to him. Tyler wasn't listening and just kept staring at me. Then he turned and walked off the stage. His lawyers followed. Reporters rushed after him. He didn't look back.

The moderator was trying to restore order. "Shareholders, please, we need to—" But no one was listening. The celebration was overwhelming, people hugging, crying, laughing.

I just stood there. 52.3%. After six weeks, after seven years since Leo died. We won. My legs gave out. I sat down hard. Jessica knelt next to me. "You okay?"

I couldn't answer, couldn't speak, just sat there as the ballroom erupted around me. We won.

Someone was pushing through the crowd, a reporter, camera crew behind her. "Ms. Parker! How does it feel to win?"

I looked up and couldn't form words.

"What's your message to Tyler Carrington?"

Jessica pulled me up. "No interviews, not now." She led me through the crowd, past celebrating shareholders, past reporters, past cameras, out into the hallway. The hotel corridor was quiet, cold, real. I leaned against the wall and slid down to the floor. "Olivia?" Jessica knelt next to me. "Talk to me."

"We won."

"We won."

"52.3%."

"52.3%." Jessica's face was wet with tears. "So close. If 2.3% had gone the other way—"

"But they didn't." I looked at her, really looked. "We won."

"We won." We sat there in the hallway, the celebration noise muffled through the walls.

After a minute, Sarah and Amanda found us, Noreen right behind them. Sarah sat down on my other side, didn't say anything, just took my hand. Amanda was still crying. "I can't believe it. I actually can't believe it."

"Vanguard voted for us," Noreen said. "I just talked to their lead manager. They said Jessica's speech convinced them, that Tyler's rebuttal about 'voting with your heads' felt dismissive."

"What about BlackRock?" Jessica asked.

"For us. Fidelity too. The institutional investors carried us over." Noreen sat down across from us. "Without them, we would've lost. It was that close."

My phone buzzed. Linda. I answered. "We won."

"I know. I watched the livestream. Grace has been sitting at the window all morning asking when you'd be done."

The words broke through the shock. Grace. Waiting, watching for me. "I'm coming home right now."

"She made you a picture, a flower. She's been holding it since breakfast, waiting to give it to you."

My throat got tight. "Tell her I'll be home in three hours."

"She keeps asking if it's real this time, if you're really done."

"I'm really done. Tell her I'm really done."

"Okay." Linda's voice got soft. "Olivia?"

"Yeah?"

"I'm proud of you." She hung up.

I looked at the others. "I need to go."

"There's a press conference in an hour," Noreen said. "We need everyone there. This is history."

"I can't. I promised Grace—"

"Just one hour," Amanda said. "One press conference. Then go."

I thought about Grace at the window, holding a flower picture, waiting to see if this time I'd keep my promise. "No. I need to go now."

Jessica studied my face, then nodded. "Go. Be with your daughter. We'll handle the press."

"You sure?"

"You earned this. Both the victory and going home." She pulled me into a hug. "Thank you for fighting, for being here, for everything."

Amanda hugged me next, then Sarah, then Noreen. "We did this together," Sarah said. "All of us."

I grabbed my bag and headed for the exit. The lobby was chaos. Reporters everywhere, cameras, shareholders celebrating. I pushed through, out the revolving doors, into New York sunlight, and got a taxi. "Airport, please. As fast as you can."

The driver pulled into traffic. I looked back at the Hilton, at the building where we'd just made history, where Tyler Carrington lost everything, where four women took back what he'd stolen.

My phone kept buzzing: texts, calls, media requests. I ignored them all and just watched New York pass by the window. Buildings, streets and normal life. The fight was over. Tyler lost. We won. And I was going home to Grace.

Finally, I was going home.

Two days later, Phoenix Rising Partners officially took control of Carrington Media. Tyler was removed from the board, his voting rights suspended, his office cleared out. The company was renamed Veritas Media. New mission statement, new leadership, new purpose.

Jessica became CEO, Amanda COO, Sarah General Counsel, Noreen Board Chair, and me? Board member, ten percent owner, home in Millfield.

They didn't need me in New York, didn't need me on TV, didn't need me fighting anymore. They just needed my vote once a month, my support, my belief that four survivors could transform a three-hundred-million-dollar company into something good. I could do that from my kitchen table, while Grace sorted her cereal by color, while Linda made coffee, while life became small and normal and safe.

The first board meeting was June 15th. Video conference. I logged in from home. Grace was at Linda's. The house was quiet. Jessica appeared on screen. "Everyone ready?"

Six faces. The board of Veritas Media. Four survivors. Two independent directors. Tyler's empire, rebuilt, reclaimed, renamed.

"First order of business," Jessica said, "hiring our investigative team. We've identified three journalists from major outlets, all interested in joining and all committed to accountability journalism."

She pulled up profiles. Names I recognized, Pulitzer winners, real journalists.

Susan Marsh will be Managing Editor. She'll build the investigative unit. The first story will be about gang corruption in Cleveland: the network that killed Leo Parker, the politicians who protected them.

My chest got tight. "Leo's story?"

"Yes, Leo's story," Jessica confirmed.

"When?"

"Four months. Susan needs time to verify everything, interview sources, build an airtight case."

Four months. By October, Leo's story would be public, his name in articles, his death meaning something beyond tragedy.

"Thank you," I said, "for making this the first story."

Jessica nodded. "It's why we're here, to tell stories that powerful people tried to bury."

The meeting continued: budgets, hiring, strategy. All important, all necessary. But I was somewhere else, thinking about Leo, about Grace, about Linda, about coming home, finally, after everything.

The meeting ended at 7:47 PM. I closed my laptop and sat in the quiet house. Grace was coming home tomorrow. First night in our new house, three blocks from Linda, three bedrooms, yellow paint in Grace's room, safe neighborhood, good schools.

Normal life, small life, the life I'd been running from since Leo died. But maybe normal was enough. Maybe small was victory. Maybe choosing the living was the whole point.

I picked up my phone and texted Linda: *Thank you. For everything. For keeping Grace safe while I fought. For never giving up on me.*

Her response came immediately: *You won. Now stay won. Be her mother. Be present. Be here.*

I will. Promise.

And this time, I meant it. This time, I'd keep it.

That night, alone in the new house, I went to the room that would be my office, empty except for boxes. One box labeled "Leo."

I opened it: photos, letters, the compass Dad gave me, the evidence from the trial, all of it. I picked up the photo from Leo's nightstand, the two of us at six and four, backyard, summer, before everything broke.

"We won," I whispered. "Not the way you deserved, not fast enough to save you, but we won. Tyler's gone. Margaret's gone. Your story's getting told."

Silence. No ghost. No voice. Just me and the past. "I'm going to be better now, for Grace, for Linda, for everyone who's still here. I'm going to stop fighting and start living."

I put the photo back, closed the box, left it in the corner. Tomorrow I'd unpack. Tomorrow Grace would arrive. Tomorrow normal life would start. But tonight, I said goodbye. To the fight, to revenge, to Leo, to everything that had kept me running for seven years. I was done, finally, completely done.

And standing there in the empty room, I felt something I hadn't felt since Leo died: peace. Not happiness, not closure, just peace, like the war was finally over, like I could finally rest.

Chapter Twelve

His Name Everywhere

Eighteen months later, I woke up to Grace climbing into my bed. "Mama, it's morning."

6:47 AM. Tuesday. October light coming through the curtains.

"I know, baby. What do you want for breakfast?"

"Pancakes. With the faces." She meant the ones where I used chocolate chips for eyes and a banana smile.

"Okay. Pancakes with faces."

We went downstairs. I made coffee while Grace set out her placemat, the one with dinosaurs she'd picked out at Target three months ago. Normal morning. Normal life, the kind Leo never got to have.

My phone was on the counter. Seventeen missed calls, thirty-four texts. That wasn't normal. I opened the messages: Jessica, Amanda, Sarah, Noreen, Linda, all within the last hour.

Jessica: *CALL ME NOW*

Amanda: *OH MY GOD, OLIVIA*

Sarah: *It's happening. It's really happening.*

Linda: *Turn on the news. I'm coming over.*

My hands started shaking. I opened my news app. The notifications loaded.

BREAKING: Ohio Senator Tied to Gang Money

EXCLUSIVE: Senator Brennan Funded by Criminal Network

VERITAS MEDIA INVESTIGATION: The Senator's Secret

I clicked the main story. The headline filled my screen.

"The Senator's Secret: How Gang Money Funded a Political Career And Who Paid the Price" *By Susan Marsh, Managing Editor, Veritas Media*

I had to sit down. "Mama?" Grace looked up from her dinosaur placemat. "You okay?"

"Yeah, baby. Just give me one second."

I started reading.

Between 2012 and 2019, Ohio State Senator Brennan received $847,000 in campaign contributions from businesses connected to a violent gang network operating in Cleveland, the same network responsible for at least 47 murders during that period.

My vision blurred. I kept reading.

One of those murders was 19-year-old Leo Parker.

Leo's name, right there, in the second paragraph, in an article the whole world could see.

Parker, a homeless teenager, had witnessed a gang murder outside Club Vertical on April 14, 2014. What happened next would cost him his life but not for the reasons anyone suspected.

Wait. My hands started shaking.

Parker didn't just witness the murder. He collected evidence, photographed gang members, documented their operations at multiple locations, and on April 17, 2014, the day before his death, he walked into Cleveland Police Department's Fourth District and tried to file a report.

No. No no no.

According to documents obtained by Veritas Media, Parker's report was flagged by a desk sergeant with ties to Senator Brennan's office. Within hours, Brennan's chief of staff was alerted.

Within twelve hours, the gang had Parker's name, description, and last known location.

My phone slipped from my hands, clattering on the floor. Linda picked it up and started reading where I'd stopped. Her face went white.

Parker was killed not just because he witnessed a murder. He was killed because he also tried to do the right thing, because he walked into a police station believing the system would protect him, because a corrupt senator and a dirty cop handed a nineteen-year-old boy to the people he was trying to expose.

"Oh my God." Linda's voice broke. "Oh my God, Olivia."

I couldn't breathe. Couldn't think.

All these years. All these years I have been wrong. Initially, I thought Leo died because he didn't have $8,000, then later, because he saw something he shouldn't have. Random. Wrong place, wrong time. But he didn't just see it; he tried to stop it.

He went to the police. He believed someone would help him. He believed the system worked, and they killed him for it.

Sergeant McCarthy, the officer who took Parker's report, received $15,000 two weeks after Parker's death. The payment came through a shell company connected to Senator Brennan's *campaign. McCarthy retired six months later. He declined to comment for this story.*

Linda kept reading aloud, her voice shaking.

Leo came to us with everything," former Detective Rivera told Veritas Media. Rivera was assigned to the Fourth District in 2014 but never saw Parker's report. "McCarthy buried it, made sure it never got entered into the system, made sure no detective ever saw it. That kid walked in asking for help, and we handed him a death sentence.

The room was spinning. Leo called me the night before he went to the police, trying to tell me he was doing something brave, something dangerous, trying to tell me he needed backup, and I didn't answer.

He went alone to that police station, believing someone would protect him, believing the right thing mattered.

I couldn't speak, could barely see through the tears. Linda's legs gave out, and she sat down hard on the kitchen floor next to me. "He tried." Her voice was barely a whisper. "He tried to do exactly what we tell kids to do: go to the police, report the crime."

"And they murdered him for it." The words came out wrong, broken. "They murdered him because he trusted the system."

Grace slid off her chair, came over to us, two women sitting on the kitchen floor, both of us crying. "Mama?" She touched my face with small hands. "Why are you crying?"

I pulled her onto my lap, held her so tight. "Because I just found out something about Uncle Leo."

"What?"

"He was braver than I ever knew, braver than anyone ever knew."

Linda was still reading the article, scrolling down. "There's more. Listen to this." Her voice shook as she read:

Parker's evidence, the photographs and notes he brought to the police station, disappeared with his report. But Parker had made copies. He'd hidden a backup set at a storage locker, along with a handwritten note: "If something happens to me, please give this to my sister Olivia. She'll know what to do."

My chest cracked open.

Parker's storage locker sat untouched for three years. When the bill went unpaid, the facility auctioned its contents in 2017. The evidence was presumed lost. It wasn't until 2019, when investor David Keller began investigating Carrington Media, that Parker's evidence resurfaced. Keller traced it through auction records, purchased it from a collector, and digitized every-

thing as part of his investigation into Margaret Carrington's money laundering operations.

But Keller had encrypted portions of his investigative archive before his murder. After federal prosecutors used accessible files to convict Margaret and Tyler Carrington, forensic specialists spent eighteen months working to recover the encrypted data. They successfully retrieved Parker's evidence (photographs, notes, and documentation) connecting a Cleveland gang network to Senator Brennan's office.

"Steve found it," Linda said, crying hard. "Steve gave Keller's files to the FBI. They used what they could access to get Margaret, but Leo's evidence was locked in the encrypted files. It took them eighteen months to break through. That's why it's breaking now. That's why we're only learning the truth now."

I couldn't speak, couldn't process. Leo's note: *She'll know what to do.* He trusted me, even after I didn't answer his call, even after I deleted his messages. He still believed I'd come for him. And seven years later, I did.

"Read me the rest," I whispered. "All of it. I need to hear all of it."

Linda pulled me close. Grace tucked between us, and she read the whole thing out loud: about Senator Brennan accepting blood money, about him blocking forty-seven murder investigations, about him being warned when Leo tried to come forward, about how he personally called the gang's lawyer, about how he made sure Leo Parker died alone in that alley, about how Leo's evidence... the evidence he died protecting... finally brought them all down. Brennan, Margaret, the gangs, the whole corrupt system.

By the time Linda finished reading, we were all crying, even Grace, who didn't understand but felt it anyway, felt the weight of what Leo had done, what it cost him, what it meant.

"He wasn't just a victim," Linda said. "He was a whistle-blower, a real one, just like Steve, just like everyone who came after."

"He was nineteen." My voice broke. "He was homeless and scared and nineteen, and he still walked into that police station believing it would matter."

"It did matter." Linda grabbed my face, made me look at her. "It took seven years, but it mattered. Everything he did mattered."

Grace wiped my tears with her small hands. "Uncle Leo was really brave?"

"The bravest person I ever knew."

"Like you, Mama?" The words destroyed me. "No, baby. I learned it from him."

My phone was buzzing again. Dozens of messages. The article going viral. Leo's name trending. His story everywhere. But I didn't care about any of that. I only cared about one thing: Leo died believing someone would help him, believing the system worked, believing his big sister would know what to do with the evidence he left behind. And somehow, impossibly, through David Keller and seven years and a thousand broken pieces... He'd been right.

My phone rang. Jessica. I answered, my voice broken. "Did you see—"

"Everyone's seeing it. Fifteen million views already. Every major outlet is picking it up. #JusticeForLeo is trending worldwide." Jessica was crying too. "We did it, Olivia. We actually did it."

"How?"

"Susan's been working on this for eight months, since we took over Veritas, using all of Keller's evidence, all of Leo's documentation, building the case brick by brick." She paused. "Your brother was an incredible investigator. He documented everything: names, dates, transactions, photographs. If he'd lived, he would've been—"

"But he didn't live."

"No, but his work did, and now everyone knows it."

We stayed on the phone, not saying much, just breathing together. The weight of eighteen months settling into something that felt like peace.

"Turn on CNN," Jessica said. "Brennan's about to make a statement."

I hung up and found the remote. Senator Brennan was at a podium, red-faced, sweating, surrounded by lawyers. "These allegations are completely false. This is a politically motivated smear campaign by an activist media company—"

A reporter interrupted. "Senator, what about the bank records? The emails showing you were warned about Leo Parker three days before he was murdered?"

"Fabricated. All of it."

"The FBI has confirmed they're investigating—"

"I never took money from gangs. I never blocked investigations. This is a vendetta by people who want to destroy me politically—"

Another reporter: "Will you resign?"

"Absolutely not. I'm innocent. I will be vindicated—"

"Senator, Leo Parker was nineteen years old when he was murdered. He was homeless. He was trying to expose corruption. Do you have any comment about his death?"

Brennan's face went white. "I—I'm not going to comment on specific individuals—"

"So you won't comment on the teenager whose evidence is being used to investigate you?"

"I have nothing to say about that."

"Will you resign?" Another reporter asked it again.

Brennan walked away from the podium. The cameras followed him, reporters shouting questions. He looked smaller than he had at the start, shrunken, defeated. Linda turned off the TV. "He'll resign by end of day."

"How do you know?"

"Because that's what guilty men do when they can't lie anymore. They run."

The morning passed in a blur of calls from reporters, emails from people who'd known Leo, messages from strangers who'd read the article and wanted to say his name mattered. One email made me cry all over again.

My brother was homeless and killed in Phoenix in 2016. No one cared, no one investigated, and no one even kept his body at the morgue. They cremated him as a John Doe. Reading about Leo made me feel like maybe my brother's death mattered too. Thank you for not giving up. - Sarah M., Phoenix AZ

Linda read it over my shoulder. "That's what Leo's story is doing: giving voice to all the forgotten ones."

"It's too much." I wiped my eyes. "I can't—I can't process this."

"You don't have to process it today. Just feel it. That's enough."

Grace came over. "Mama, you're still crying."

"I know, baby. I'm sorry."

"It's okay." She climbed onto my lap. "Gamma says crying is good sometimes, gets the sad out."

"Where'd you learn that?"

"Gamma told me, when I cried about my fish dying."

Linda smiled. "Smart kid."

We sat there, Grace warm in my lap, Linda's hand on my shoulder, the three of us together.

By noon, Senator Brennan had resigned. By 2 PM, the FBI had arrested him.

I made Linda turn on the TV. I needed to see it, needed to watch justice happen with my own eyes: Brennan being led out of his office, hands cuffed behind his back, cameras flashing, reporters shouting. He looked nothing like the confident man from that morning. He looked broken, caught, finished.

"That's for Leo," Linda said quietly.

I couldn't speak, just watched as they put him in the car, as the door closed, as he disappeared. Seven years, and now this: real handcuffs, real arrest, real consequences.

Grace was watching too. "They got him, Mama?"

"They got him."

"Good." She went back to coloring, drew a flower with careful concentration. "This is for Uncle Leo, for when we visit him."

I hadn't told her Leo had a grave, that we'd moved him two years ago from the unmarked plot to a real cemetery with a real headstone that said his name.

"How did you know Uncle Leo has a grave?"

"Gamma told me. She said we could visit sometime, put flowers there." Grace added petals to her drawing. "Can we go today?"

"After school tomorrow, okay?"

"Okay." She colored in silence for a minute, then: "Mama? Can you tell me about Uncle Leo? Like, what he was really like?"

The question caught me off guard. We'd talked about Leo before, but never like this, never with Grace really listening, really wanting to know. I sat down next to her. "What do you want to know?"

"Was he nice?"

"He was really nice. He was funny. He made me laugh a lot when I was little."

"What did he laugh about?"

"Silly things. He used to make up songs about our cat, really bad songs that didn't rhyme, but they were funny."

Grace smiled, added a stem to her flower. "Did he like dinosaurs?"

My throat got tight. "Yeah, baby, he loved dinosaurs."

"Really?"

He had a green stuffed dinosaur named Rex and carried him everywhere, even when he got older. Rex was his best friend.

"Like my bunny?"

"Exactly like your bunny. When Leo was scared or sad, he'd hold Rex. It made him feel safe."

Grace's eyes got wide. "What happened to Rex?"

I had to think. Where was Rex? Then I remembered. "He's in Leo's room, on his bed. I kept all of Leo's special things."

"Can I see Rex someday?"

"Yeah. We can go look at Leo's room together. I'll show you Rex and tell you stories about Uncle Leo."

"Okay." Grace went back to coloring.

After a couple of minutes: "Mama?"

"Yeah?"

"Do I have a daddy?"

The question hit me like cold water. The transition was so abrupt from Leo to her father, but that's how kids' minds worked, connecting dots in ways that made sense to them. "What made you think about that?"

"Because Uncle Leo had a dad who died, but I never met my daddy." Grace's voice was matter-of-fact, curious, not sad. "Maya at school has a daddy who picks her up sometimes. Do I have one?"

My chest tightened. "Yeah, baby. You have a daddy."

"Where is he?"

I chose my words carefully. "He's in jail. He did some bad things and hurt some people, so he had to go to jail for a long time."

Grace absorbed this, her crayon still moving across the paper. "Did he hurt you?"

"Yeah, he hurt me a long time ago, before you were born."

"Did you have to fight him?"

"Yeah..."

"Did you win?"

"We won, and he's staying in jail for a really long time, until you're all grown up."

"Good." She kept coloring, added more details to her flower. "Mama?"

"Yeah?"

"I don't think I want a daddy."

The words hit me hard. "Why not?"

"Because if my daddy hurt you, then he's a bad person, and I don't want a bad person to be my daddy." She looked up at me, her eyes clear and certain. "I just want you and Gamma. Is that okay?"

I could barely breathe. "Yeah, baby. That's more than okay."

"Good." She went back to her flower. After a minute: "Can we have mac and cheese for lunch?" Just like that, from Uncle Leo to daddies to lunch. Five-year-olds.

I made her mac and cheese. We ate on the couch watching her favorite movie, a normal afternoon, a normal life, but different somehow, because Grace knew now, knew about Leo, knew about her father, knew the truth in pieces she could handle, and she'd chosen us, chosen me and Linda, chosen the family we'd built.

That was enough, more than enough.

That evening, after Grace was in bed, Linda and I sat in the living room watching the news. Senator Brennan's arraignment was the lead story on every channel, charged with corruption, conspiracy, obstruction of justice, and accessory to murder.

"Accessory to murder?" I looked at Linda. "They're charging him with Leo's death?"

"The emails show Brennan knew about the hit. Knew Parker was collecting evidence. Knew he was a threat. His office gave tacit approval for the gang to 'handle it.'" Linda's face was grim. "Prosecutors think they can prove he knew Leo would be killed."

"How long could he get?"

"Twenty years minimum. Maybe life."

I couldn't speak, just stared at the TV. Twenty years. For Leo.

My phone buzzed. Unknown number. I answered. "Hello?"

"Is this Olivia Parker?" A woman's voice, professional but warm.

"Yes."

"This is Susan Marsh. I wrote the article about your brother."

My breath caught. "I—thank you. Thank you for telling his story, for making people see him."

"I need to thank you. Without your evidence, without Keller's documentation, without your seven years of refusing to let go, none of this would have happened." She paused. "Your brother was remarkable, Olivia. His investigation was meticulous, professional-grade. If he'd lived, he could've been an incredible journalist."

"He was homeless. He was nineteen. He was barely surviving."

"And he still documented everything. Names. Dates. Transactions. Photographs with timestamps. He knew what he had. He knew it mattered." Susan's voice got softer. "We found something in Keller's files, a phone record three days before Leo died. He made calls. Do you know who he called?"

My throat closed. "Me. He called me."

Silence.

"What did you talk about?"

"I didn't answer." The words came out broken. "I saw it was him and I—I ignored it. I thought he wanted money for drugs. I thought he was being dramatic, so I didn't answer."

"I'm so sorry."

"I've spent seven years trying to make up for not answering that call, seven years wondering what he would've said in those forty-seven seconds."

"You did make up for it. This story... It's not just about Brennan. It's about what happens when we ignore the vulnerable, when we dismiss people like Leo because they're homeless or addicted or inconvenient." Susan paused. "You made sure people couldn't ignore him anymore. That matters. It matters more than one phone call."

After we hung up, I just sat there for a while. Linda handed me a mug of tea. Strong, sweet, the way I liked it. "You okay?"

"Susan said Leo called me three days before he died." I took a sip. The tea was hot, grounding. "What do you say when you know you're going to die?"

"Maybe he wasn't trying to say goodbye. Maybe he just wanted to hear your voice."

The thought broke me. I started crying again and couldn't stop. Linda pulled me close. "You answered, Olivia. For seven years. Every single day. You answered."

We sat like that for a long time, the news playing on mute, Brennan's face on every channel.

After Linda left, I went upstairs and stood outside Leo's room. The door was half-open, the way I'd left it months ago. Not a tomb, not a shrine, just a room with memories. I went in and sat on his bed. The springs creaked under my weight.

The photos were still on the wall: Leo at four, holding Rex, that green stuffed dinosaur; at ten; at fifteen; at nineteen. The progression of a life that ended too soon. Rex was still on the bed, faded green fabric, one eye missing, loved to pieces. I picked him up and held him. This had been Leo's comfort, his safe place.

On the nightstand was Grandpa's compass, the one Dad gave me before the drinking destroyed everything. The brass was tarnished, the glass cracked, but the needle still pointed north, still worked.

I picked it up, held it in one hand, Rex in the other. Three generations in my hands.

"We did it," I said to the empty room, to Leo's ghost, to the brother I'd spent seven years trying to save. "Your story broke today. Everyone knows your name now. Senator Brennan was arrested and is being charged as an accessory to your murder. The gang network is being investigated. Everything you tried to do, it worked. It all worked."

The compass was heavy. Rex was light. Tears were on my face. "I was twenty-one and drowning, and I didn't know how to help you. I didn't know you were really in danger. If I'd known... if I'd answered—"

I stopped and breathed. "But I can't change that. I can only change what I did after, and I spent seven years making sure your death mattered, making sure people knew your name, making sure the men who killed you paid for it."

I turned the compass over and read Dad's inscription: *Always find your way home. - Dad*

"You were trying to find your way home that night, and I didn't answer. But Leo—" My voice broke. "Your story made it home, finally, after seven years. Your evidence, your courage, your name, it all made it home."

I set Rex carefully back on the bed and set the compass next to him. I stood up and walked to his photos, touched the one of him at four, holding Rex. "I'm going to give her this compass when she turns thirteen, tell her it was mine, tell her it was Dad's before that, tell her it represents always finding your way home." I paused. "And I'll give her Rex too, if she wants him, so she can have a piece of you."

I walked to the door and turned back one more time. "Rest now, Leo. Your work is done. Your story is told. Twenty-two million people have read your name. Senator Brennan is going to prison. The gang network is being dismantled across six states. You changed everything."

One more thing I needed to say: "I forgive myself for not answering your call. I was twenty-one and lost and drowning in my own mess. I didn't know, but I've spent seven years making up for it." My voice was steady now, strong. "And that's enough. I forgive myself." Saying it out loud made it real, made it true. I closed the door, not all the way, just enough.

Morning came early. I spent the day cleaning, doing laundry, normal things. Grace had been talking about visiting Uncle Leo all week, ever since Linda told her about the grave.

At 2:30 PM, Linda and I drove to Grace's preschool. She ran out wearing finger paint on her sleeve and clutching a folded paper, her flower drawing. "Mama! Gamma!" She climbed into her car seat and held up the drawing. "For Uncle Leo, remember?"

"I remember, baby. We're going right now."

"Really?" Her whole face lit up.

"Really, just like I promised."

We drove to the cemetery, Grace quiet in the backseat, serious, like she understood this mattered.

Leo's headstone was simple, clean, his name, his dates. One line:

LEO PARKER1995 - 2014He tried to do the right thing

Grace walked up to it slowly, touched the letters with one finger. "Uncle Leo."

"That's right, baby."

She carefully unfolded her drawing, purple and yellow petals, a green stem. She'd worked so hard on it. "I made this at school, for you."

She placed it at the base of the stone, smoothed it flat, making sure it looked perfect. I knelt down beside her, pulled something from my bag, a small green dinosaur, not Rex. I was saving Rex for Grace, but a new one, like Rex, green and soft.

"For you," I said to the stone, "so you're not alone."

Grace's eyes went wide. "Like Rex?"

"Just like Rex, so Uncle Leo has a dinosaur too."

She thought about this, then nodded, like it made perfect sense. "Uncle Leo needs a dinosaur in heaven."

Linda put her hand on the headstone. Her voice was soft. "You can rest now, sweetie. Your sister made sure everyone knows your name, made sure your death mattered, made sure no one forgets."

Grace looked up at me. "Mama fought the bad people?"

"Yes, baby, Mama fought them and won."

"Good." She touched the dinosaur, adjusted it so it sat better. "Is Uncle Leo happy now?"

My throat closed up. "Yeah, I think he is."

We stood there in silence, the October wind cold, the leaves falling, the sun bright. Grace held my hand on one side, Linda's on the other, three generations, still standing, still here. Finally, Linda spoke. "What now?"

"What do you mean?"

"The fight's over. Tyler's in prison, Margaret's in prison, Brennan's in prison. Leo's story is told, the bad guys lost, you won." Linda looked at me. "What do you do now?"

I looked down at Grace. She was kneeling now, talking quietly to the headstone, telling Leo about her day at school, about the painting she made, about her friend Emma who shared her crackers at snack time.

"I'll go home," I said. "Make dinner. Help Grace with homework. Read her three books instead of two. Tell her stories about Leo and Rex. Wake up tomorrow and do it again. Live the life Leo never got to have."

"That's it?"

"That's everything."

Linda smiled. "Perfect answer."

Grace tugged at my hand. "Can we come back? Visit Uncle Leo again?"

"Anytime you want, baby."

"With more flowers?"

"With more flowers."

She nodded, satisfied, then kissed her hand and pressed it to the stone. "Bye, Uncle Leo. Love you."

We walked back to the car, Grace between us, swinging our hands, still talking about the dinosaur, about coming back next week, about making another flower drawing. Just a normal afternoon, a normal family, doing normal things.

Leo's story was told. His name was remembered. His death changed everything, and somewhere, somehow, I believed he knew it, believed he was proud, believed he was finally at peace, running with his dinosaur through fields of light.

Free. Forever.

Chapter Thirteen

Author's Note

THANK YOU FOR FINISHING Olivia's story.

If you made it through all five books, you know what it's like to watch someone break every promise they made and still find a way forward. That's not fiction. That's recovery. That's real life.

I wrote these books because I needed to tell the truth about addiction and family trauma. The kind of truth that doesn't fit in polite conversation, the kind that makes you uncomfortable because you recognize yourself in it.

Olivia's fight is over, but if you're not ready to leave this world behind, I have more stories for you.

Visit https://selfcarejourneybooks.com/ to find my other books about addiction, recovery, and the messy work of becoming someone you're proud to be. Each one tells a different truth. Each one might hit you exactly when you need it.

*https://selfcarejourne
ybooks.com/*

And if this series meant something to you, please leave a review. It helps other people find these books when they need them most.

Thank you for trusting me with your time.

With gratitude,

Howard Kane

https://selfcarejourneybooks.com/

265

This page was intentionally left blank.

266

This page was intentionally left blank.

This page was intentionally left blank.

268

This page was intentionally left blank.